HEAVENLY WISHES

Heavenly Wishes

CAROL A CAMPBELL

*To My Mom & Dad
Here's To Chasing Dreams &
Finding My Way Back Home!*

Copyright © 2024 by Carol Campbell
All rights reserved. No part of this book may be reproduced in any manner whatsoever without written permission except in the case of brief quotations embodied in critical articles and reviews.
First Printing, 2024

Special Thanks:

A heartfelt thanks to the following brave volunteers who allowed their names to appear as fictional characters in this fictional story:

Micky Vermooch	Dondi & Cindy Morrow
Loretta Cobb	Mike & Kathy Berry
Gail Norris Terry	Steve Strittmatter
Jill Ecker	Jason Riesenbeck
Matilda Sharbino	Terrie Lawson
Lena White	Amanda Sheppard
Tricia Grigar	Evelyn Danner
Patricia Noack	Tanya Corkern
Margie Richard	Stephanie Dawn Terry
Brenda Menifee	Catrina McSpadden
Emmett Johnson	John J. Wolfe
LaDonna Koehne	Laurrie McBride
Cindy Blevins	Taylor McCray
Jeffery Hopper	Shannon (Shanster) Wright
Melissa Newman Staggs	Stefanie (Firecracker) Jordan

Your willingness to be a part of this tale has helped bring Bayou Vista to life.

Prologue

Bayou Vista ain't much of a town, but it's all I've ever known. Folks here say the swamp's got secrets. Whispers carried on the wind through the cypress trees. Lately, those whispers have turned into shouts, louder than the crickets at night. Four women have gone missing in a month. My teacher, Mrs. Staggs, says it's the devil's work. Others say it's a serial killer, a monster lurking in the shadows. But I don't care much about monsters, not the kind that hides under beds. My monsters are real, and they live right here in this house.

I'm Loretta. I'm ten years old, and small for my age. My stepdad, Roy, makes sure I never forget it. He's got a temper like a storm, all fists and fury, and I'm his favorite punching bag. My Mama disappeared when I was four. Roy said she died, but I can't remember much about her at that age. He's meaner than a snake, and when he drinks, which is always, he turns into something worse. I keep my head down, stay quiet, and dream of a way out.

There's talk in town about a new store on Main Street—Micky's Magical Things. The name alone makes my heart flutter-Magic. The kind that can make monsters disappear and dreams come true. I haven't been inside yet, but I've seen the window displays filled with shimmering trinkets and old books that look like they hold secrets. Maybe, just maybe, there's something in there that can help me. A spell to make Roy go away. A charm to keep me safe. Anything.

The whole town's on edge, but I've got my own worries. I hear the whispers about the missing women when I sneak into town, people talking in hushed voices outside the diner and on the church steps. They say it ain't safe for a girl to be out alone, but home's no safer. I figure if the devil's really out there, I might just stand a chance against him. I've been fighting my own battles for as long as I can remember.

Tomorrow, I'm gonna sneak into Micky's. I've got a few coins saved up, hidden in the hollow of my bedpost. Enough, I hope, to buy something magical. Something powerful. Something that'll change everything. Maybe it's just a dream, but it's all I've got. And in a town where shadows hide secrets, and danger lurks in every corner, dreams are worth holding onto. Even if they're all you have.

And this, well, this is my story...

~ 1 ~

COME OUT, COME OUT, WHEREVER YOU ARE!

"Loretta," he screamed from the front door. The sound of his voice echoed through the house, sending chills down my spine. I could feel my heart pounding as I desperately searched for a place to hide.

The front yard was dimly lit in the early morning darkness, and the thorny leaf bush at the corner of the house provided the perfect cover for me. I scurried behind it, careful not to make a sound. The dirt beneath my feet was damp from the recent rain, adding an extra layer of difficulty to my escape.

As I pushed aside the branches of the bush, I found myself surrounded by dense foliage. Louisiana's high humidity made my skin sticky, clinging to the leaves that pierced my body. There was no need for me to worry about that now. My only concern now was staying hidden until he left.

Why couldn't he just leave without waking me for once?

The porch wood floor echoed with the sound of his old work boots.

Laughing, he taunts, "Come out, come out, wherever you are."

Time seemed to stand still as I crouched behind the bush, waiting for the right moment to make my escape. Every nerve in my body was on edge, and my fingers trembled with anticipation. I could feel the sweat trickling down my forehead. Mud covered my bare feet and my blue cotton pajamas.

"I don't have time for this crap today," he grumbled as he walked across the porch to go inside. "I'm late for work."

Finally, the sound of his footsteps faded as he made his way through the house and out the back door. The house was silent once again. I cautiously emerged from behind the bush, my heart still pounding in my chest. It had been a close call, and my mind raced with thoughts of what could have happened if I had been discovered.

We live on a corner, and our garage is in the rear, facing another road. From where I stood, I could see the driveway, and I watched as he got into his old black Dodge truck. The engine roared to life, and the vibrations spread through the ground beneath me. The sound was so loud that it almost masked the pounding of my own heart.

I watched, almost statuette-like, as he pulled out of the driveway and sped down the street. The sound of his engine grew fainter and fainter, until it was completely gone. Only then did I allow myself to relax and exhale. My relief washed over me like a wave. It was over, at least, for now.

As I stood there, I searched for a new place to hide. The prickly leaf bush shielded me for now, but I knew it was only a matter of time before he would find my hiding place.

"What on earth are you doing, honey?" a woman shouted from next door.

Turning around quickly, I saw my neighbor next door sitting on the porch. She moved in two years ago, and I had never talked to her. Roy's number one rule: Don't talk to anyone.

She motioned to me with her hand, saying, "Come here, honey."

I slowly make my way over to her house.

All the houses on the street are the same: triangle-shaped, wood-framed, with large railed porches and three giant concrete steps. All of them are painted white, but not hers. It stands out, painted yellow with lime green trim.

Bright blue pots filled with vibrant flowers and hot pink chairs caught my attention as I approached the colorful porch.

As I climb the steps, the woman stands up and gestures to me again. "It's okay, sit down," she says, her voice filled with concern. She points to one of the hot pink wicker chairs. It's a comfortable-looking chair, but it's definitely not like anything else in the neighborhood.

I hesitate for a moment, unsure of what to say.

"Really, honey, it's okay," she said with a smile as she sat back down.

In my house, everything is strictly off-limits when it comes to flowers or the color pink. It's deemed a sign of weakness, I thought as I took a seat on the chair.

"Honey," she said as she sipped her coffee and stared at me with her piercing green eyes.

"Y..yes, ma'am," I nervously stuttered.

"Oh, there's no need for all that formality," she chuckles. "That makes me feel older than I am. My name is Gail Norris Terry, and you can call me Gail," she said with a wink. "What's your name?"

"Loretta Cobb, but you can call me Loretta."

The red-haired lady burst into laughter, "You're quite a character."

I giggle, even though I wasn't trying to be funny.

Suddenly, the laughter stopped, and a serious expression formed on Gail's beautiful face. "Why is your dad always yelling at you?"

"That's not my dad," I blurted out defensively. "He's my stepdad, Roy."

"Oh," she sighed, raising her eyebrows curiously. "Where's your mom?"

"She's dead."

Her face suddenly became soft. "I'm sorry, honey."

"It's okay. I don't really remember much about my mom." I watched her nervously gulp her coffee as she studied me up and down.

"Where's your dad?"

"I never met my dad?" The look of shock on her face was apparent as she glanced over to my house and then back at me.

"How old are you?"

"I'm ten years old," I quickly replied. "How old are you?"

"You're not supposed to ask a woman her age," she chuckled.

"Why not? You asked me how old I am."

"Fair enough," she grinned. "I'm thirty-eight."

She's around the same age as my mother would have been.

"Well, Loretta," she nervously sighed.

I could tell by the way she fidgeted and twitched her mouth that she was struggling to spit out the remaining questions, and I'm sure she would have a lot of them by the way she was staring at me.

"Why haven't I ever seen you outside playing? Don't you have any friends?"

"I'm not allowed to play outside, and my friends are not allowed to come over."

"What?" she shrieked. "How ridiculous is that?" She places her cup on the bright orange-painted table beside her and leans toward me. I could feel her hands shaking as she put them on my knees.

I started to jerk away, but I didn't want to make her any more suspicious than she already was, even though I knew what question was next.

"What's going on in your house, Loretta?" her voice cracked. "Why can't you play outside, and why is he always screaming at the top of his lungs? It is clear he drinks because I have seen him several times passed out on the porch with beer cans all over the place."

I can't tell her. He threatened to kill me if I told anyone. I thought as I looked into her eyes.

I quickly stood up and ran off the porch.

"Where are you going?" she yelled.

"I need to get ready for school," I shouted, running up the steps to my house.

"But I can help you," she shouted again, her voice cracking with concern.

I ignored her pleas and rushed inside, locking the door behind me.

~ 2 ~

MY BEST FRIEND, JILL

Looking at the time, I realized I had exactly thirty minutes to get ready for school and make it there on time. I was hoping that my best friend, Jill Ecker, would still be at her house waiting for me. We had been inseparable since we met in first grade. Everyone thinks we're sisters because we look so much alike. Both of us have long blonde hair, but her eyes are blue, and mine are brown. She lives only one block away from my school, and our short morning walks had become a ritual that we both enjoyed for the last four years.

After quickly getting dressed, I rushed out of my house, anxious to meet up with Jill. As I closed the door behind me, I couldn't help but glance over at Gail's house. The same two women were sitting on the porch with her, drinking coffee as they do every morning. But today, to my surprise, they stared intently at me, peering over their cups raised to the bottom of their chins, judging me silently. Most of the time, I leave the house unnoticed, except for the neighbor across the street, John Wolfe, shouting at me to watch for cars when crossing the road. He's the priest at St. Theresa Catholic Church, the town's only church.

I'm sure Gail must have filled them in on everything that happened this morning.

The sight caught me off guard, and it made me feel uncomfortable. I wanted to look away, but I couldn't tear myself away from their penetrating gazes. The tension in the air was thick, and I could feel my cheeks burning with shame.

Suddenly, breaking the silence, Gail shouted, "Honey, come over after school. I want to talk to you."

My heartbeat quickened, and I wasn't sure how to respond. I decided to ignore her, so I scurried off the porch and down the road without saying a word.

As I walked towards Jill's house, I wondered what Gail might have said about me. Did she tell them about me hiding this morning and my stepdad looking for me? Did she add to the story about him having a drinking problem? Was it just my imagination, or were they truly judging me? I couldn't dwell on it for long because it was too late now. If she's watching my house, she'll uncover the truth soon enough.

Finally, I reached Jill's house. As always, she was already waiting for me. We exchanged a quick hug and set off to school together, walking side by side as we had every morning before.

"What took you so long?" Jill asked, pulling her long hair into a ponytail.

I gave her an apologetic smile. "Sorry, my stepdad was acting crazy again this morning."

"Oh, no," she gasped. "Did he push you down again?"

I shook my head. "No, he didn't."

Suddenly, Jill stopped and grabbed me by the arm. "Loretta, you need to tell someone what he's doing."

I nervously looked away. "I can't," I whispered. "Remember what he said would happen to me."

Jill took a deep breath and hugged me.

"Yes, I remember," she whispered in my ear. "Just promise me that you will come to my house if you ever get scared. My dad won't let anything happen to you."

I couldn't help but smile as I squeezed her in return. Jill was the first person I had ever met who actually cared about me. She knew better than anyone how Roy treated me, and she had always been there for me.

"I promise," I said, my voice barely above a whisper.

Jill smiled, a radiant glow spreading across her face. "Okay," she said, her voice taking on a lighter tone. "We better hurry. Mrs. Staggs warned us that we couldn't be late today or we would miss the field trip bus."

"I forgot about that," I admitted, thinking about the fun day ahead.

We rushed towards the school, laughing and chatting along the way. We'd been looking forward to the field trip to the zoo and the museum for weeks, and we weren't about to miss it.

The anticipation grew as we approached the school gates. We could already hear the distant sound of the bus, its engine rumbling as it made its way towards us.

Mrs. Staggs, our teacher, was waiting at the gate. Her long blonde hair cascaded down her shoulders and framed her delicate face. She looked at us with her soft blue eyes and a stern look on her face. "You're just in time," she said, her voice laced with a hint of disappointment. "If you two had been any later, we would have had to leave without you."

"I'm sorry," I apologized, lowering my head and trying to find an excuse. "But..."

"My dog ran out the front door, and we had to chase after him," Jill blurted out.

My body shook with relief as I looked at Jill with a smile.

Mrs. Staggs shook her head, but we could see a hint of a smile beneath her stern demeanor. "It's fine," she said, relenting. "I hope you got your dog back in the house okay."

"Yes," Jill said, grinning back at me. "We did."

"Now, let's get on the bus and have some fun!" Mrs. Staggs patted our backs as we rushed to the bus.

As we boarded, the other students greeted us with excitement and anticipation.

"Angela," the school bus driver, Matilda Sharbino, said, her eyes twinkling with amusement. "You have a group of impatient students waiting on you."

Mrs. Staggs laughed, shaking her head as she sat down in the seat behind her. "Don't I know it," she replied.

As the bus pulled away from the school, the journey began. A fresh breeze flowed through the open windows, bringing with it a sense of liberation. For the first time in what felt like forever, I could breathe without the weight of my stepdad, Roy, and all the problems at home pressing down on me. Even if it was just for a day, it was freedom—sweet, fleeting freedom.

~ 3 ~

THE LONG WAY HOME!

The day went by way too fast. My stomach tightened as we drove back into the school's parking lot. I loved being at school. It was the only time that I felt normal and could be around my friends.

As we waited patiently for Mrs. Staggs to exit the bus, I couldn't help but notice how her eyes sparkled as she laughed with Matilda. She was one of those people who radiated happiness and positivity, always smiling and bringing joy to everyone around her.

I wish that she was my mother. My life would be so different.

"Are you daydreaming? What a fun day," Jill chirped happily, nudging my arm to snap me out of my thoughts. She gestured for me to stand up and move aside, her excitement infectious. "Do you want to take the long way home?" she asked, her eyes sparkling with the promise of more adventure.

"I'd love to," I said eagerly, jumping out of my seat.

There is an old dirt trail that begins at the edge of the schoolyard, winding through the woods that dead-end at the edge of town. Ever since the hurricane last year and now with the four missing women, the trail once popular with joggers and walkers has become obsolete. There were a lot of rumors about the trail and the old Pond, known as Preacher's Pond, located right outside of town. Many believed it to be the hunting ground of the serial killer, who might be stalking his victims there.

Jill laughed and playfully pushed me toward the exit. "My mom is helping her sister today, so I have a couple of hours before she gets home. How about you?"

"Roy never gets home before seven, so I'm good."

Mrs. Staggs smiled as we exited the bus and said, "See you guys tomorrow."

"Okay," we both replied.

With the sun shining brightly and a warm, humid breeze blowing, we hurried out of the schoolyard and turned on the old walking path.

After a few moments, Jill, with a worried look on her face, asked, "How long has it been since we've been here?"

"Over a year at least. Before the hurricane," I replied, studying her expression closely. I could tell that she was genuinely concerned. "Why?"

"Maybe we should've just walked through the neighborhood instead," she replied nervously, glancing over her shoulder.

"Why?" I asked with a grin. "Are you scared?"

Without hesitation, she blurted, "What do you think happened to all of the missing women? Do you really think that a serial killer is living in Bayou Vista?"

I hesitated for a moment, trying to gauge her reaction. "I'm not sure, but I overheard one of Roy's friends say something about the serial killer living around here, which is why he hasn't been caught. He thinks the killer blends in so well that no one notices him. He also believes that the killer is taking the women to the next town, Pelican Bay, and disposing of their bodies in the ocean from a fishing boat."

Her eyes widened. "A fishing boat?"

I nodded somberly, confirming the news. "Yes, that's what Roy's friend, Gary, said. He must have thought about it a lot to come up with all those details."

"Really," Jill muttered.

"You know Roy's friends are just as goofy as he is," I giggled.

Her voice trembling, she asked, "But he won't come after us, right?"

I hesitated again as I tried to think of something to say that would put her mind at rest. "We don't have anything to worry about because he doesn't target kids."

"That's good," she said, her voice barely above a whisper.

I hope he doesn't, I thought, my chest tightening with anxiety as I nervously glanced around. I quickened my pace, staying just a step ahead of her, hoping she wouldn't notice the worry etched on my face.

As we ventured deeper into the woods, the path became narrower and more overgrown. The trees towering above us seemed even darker and more dangerous. Jill clutched my hand tightly, her grip tightening with each step we took. It was obvious that she was still scared.

"We've been walking forever," Jill whispered, her voice barely louder than the soft crunch of leaves under our feet.

I looked up, trying to gauge the time by the sunlight flickering through the trees. It felt like hours, but I knew it was probably just a few minutes. The tension in the air was thick, making it hard to breathe. *This probably wasn't a good idea, sneaking off into the woods like this, but it's too late now.*

As we ventured further, the path became trickier. The underbrush grew denser, tangling around our legs and making it hard to move. Branches seemed to reach out like fingers, grabbing at our clothes and scratching our skin.

"Watch out," I warned, pointing at something moving on the ground on the side of us.

"Is that a snake?" she gasped.

"I hope not," I mumbled, speeding up my pace.

Just when I thought we couldn't get any deeper, we stumbled upon a fork in the trail. One path veered off to the left, disappearing into a tunnel of thick greenery, while the other continued straight, looking just as mysterious.

Jill stopped, her eyes darting between the two paths. "Which way should we go?" she asked, biting her lip.

I looked around, trying to feel brave. "I don't know. The left one looks kinda creepy, but the straight one might just lead us deeper into the woods."

Jill nodded, her face pale. "Maybe we should go back," she suggested, but I could tell she didn't really want to. Neither did I.

"We can't stop now," I said, trying to sound more confident than I felt. "Let's just pick one and see where it goes." Taking a deep breath, I pointed to the path on the left. "That one. It might be quicker."

Jill hesitated, then nodded. "Okay, let's go."

As we turned down the left path, the forest seemed to close in around us. The trees grew taller and the shadows darker. I could hear my heart pounding in my ears, each beat matching the rhythm of our footsteps. The air felt even heavier here, and every sound seemed magnified.

Suddenly, a loud crack echoed through the woods. Jill and I froze, eyes wide, staring into the darkness ahead. My heart raced as I strained to see what had made the noise. *Was it just an animal? Or something else?*

"What was that?" Jill whispered.

"I don't know, but I think we need to hurry and get out of here," I whispered back, trying to hide my fear.

Jill didn't hesitate for a moment. She swiftly hurried along the path, gripping my hand firmly and pulling me along behind her.

As we approached the end of the trail, the sparkling water of Preacher's Pond reflected the bright sun and the surroundings opened up, revealing our small town. Relief washed over us as we emerged from the darkness of the woods.

Jill let go of my hand, her tension dissipating with every step. "Thank God we're off that path," she said with a sigh of relief. "I'm glad we didn't run into the serial killer."

"Silly Jilly," I chuckled, but that was exactly what I was thinking, too.

~ 4 ~

THE TOWN OF BAYOU VISTA

The Louisiana sun beamed brightly overhead, casting a warm, golden glow upon Bayou Vista's Main Street. As we walked past Preacher's Pond and the church, I kicked a pebble along the sidewalk, my worn sneakers scuffing against the concrete. Beside me, Jill chattered away, her long ponytail bouncing with each step.

High above, gulls cry out with gusto, their wings a blur as they dance in the salty breeze, gracefully gliding through the air. The waves crashed rhythmically against the shore, their calming sound blending seamlessly with the hustle and bustle of the town.

I love the sound of the ocean. That is the only thing that I love about my house. At night, I eagerly open my bedroom window, greeted by the familiar scent of salt lingering in the air and the gentle rumble of the ocean. It's like a lullaby, singing me a bedtime story. It's as if the waves are wrapping around me, protecting me, keeping me safe and sound— shielding me from Roy's drunken rage.

I gaze down at the harbor, just beyond the church, and see a fleet of vibrant fishing boats swaying gently on the water. That's where Roy works. Despite their chipped paint and weathered nets, they still look lively and colorful. Some are docked, with workers bustling about, unloading crates brimming with shrimp and crab onto the docks.

"Where should we go first?" Jill asked.

"Let's go to C&D Kwik Stop," I suggested. "Maybe Cindy and Dondi will give us some candy."

Jill nodded eagerly.

The colorful fall flowers lining the sidewalk swayed gently in the breeze, their vibrant petals a stark contrast to the dark thoughts that often filled my mind. Main Street was a single, bustling road lined with quaint shops and familiar faces. It was a small town, but to us, it was a world of its own.

As we approached C&D Kwik Stop, the jingle of the doorbell announced our arrival. With her green eyes and golden hair elegantly secured in a bun, Cindy Morrow greeted us with a warm smile. "Well, look who it is! How are my favorite girls today?"

"We're good, Ms. Cindy," Jill chirped.

Dondi, Cindy's husband, emerged from the back, wiping his hands on a rag. "You two staying out of trouble?" he teased.

I managed a small smile. "Yes, sir."

Cindy's expression grew serious for a moment. "Listen, girls. I need you to promise me something. Stay off the old walking path, okay? Just look at all the missing women," she said, pointing at the posters hanging on the window by the door. "There's talk of a serial killer in the area. We don't want you getting hurt."

How did she know that we took the walking path? I thought as I exchanged nervous glances with Jill, but we both nodded in agreement.

"We promise," Jill said.

Dondi reached behind the counter and handed us each a candy bar. "Here, something sweet to keep you safe."

"Thank you!" we chorused before dashing back outside.

"Y'all better be careful," Cindy shouted. "There's a monster on the prowl!"

Jill softly giggled as we walked away from the store. "She's such a worry-wart," she whispered to me.

We left the store, savoring the sweet taste of chocolate as we strolled down Main Street. Passing by Shanster Travels, we saw the vivacious Shannon Wright, the owner, waving enthusiastically. Her blonde hair shimmered in the sunlight, and her sparkling blue eyes were full of energy. "Planning a trip, ladies?" she called out cheerfully from the doorway, her voice as bright as her smile.

"Not today, Ms. Shannon," I replied, giggling.

She's friends with our teacher, Mrs. Staggs, and they often go on trips together throughout the year.

Their next stop was Catrina's Closet, the local clothing store owned by Catrina McSpadden. The window display was full of colorful dresses and cute accessories. I admired a lavender dress but knew I could never afford it.

"Maybe one day," Jill said, noticing my longing gaze.

Further along, the irresistible aroma of fresh pastries led us to LaDonna's bakery, whimsically named "Frog's Delight." The owner, LaDonna Koehne, was known for her frog obsession. Inside, the shelves were lined with an assortment of frog-themed cookies, cakes, and pastries, each one crafted with meticulous detail. The cheerful, amphibian decor only added to the bakery's charm, making it a delightful stop for anyone in town.

LaDonna greeted us with a wide smile. "Hey there, sweeties!"

"Hello, Ms. LaDonna," I replied, staring at all the delicious treats.

"Try the new frog-shaped cookies," LaDonna urged, handing them each a sample. "They're toad-ally delicious."

I giggled at the pun and took a bite. The cookie melted in my mouth, and for a moment, the worries of my world faded away.

"Thank you for the cookie," Jill replied with a mouthful. "They're to croak for."

LaDonna laughed, her eyes sparkling with delight at our reactions. The warmth of her laughter made the cozy bakery feel even more inviting.

With our delicious treats in hand, we approached the center of town. We noticed a group of elderly men playing checkers at the town square. Across the street, in the heart of town, stood the courthouse, nestled between the Sheriff's office and the Mayor's office. Judge Jeffery Hopper, a stern yet fair man, often patrolled the steps, his piercing eyes missing nothing. Sheriff Emmett Johnson, a tall, muscular, black man with broad shoulders and a no-nonsense demeanor, chatted with Mayor Steve Strittmatter, a cheerful and charismatic man with a booming laugh.

Next, we wandered past Tanya's Crawfish Shack, where the smell of seasoned seafood filled the air. Tanya Corkern, the owner, was outside chatting with a customer.

"You girls hungry?" she called out, her Southern drawl thick and warm.

"Not today, Ms. Tanya," I replied.

"Okay, sweethearts! Stay safe and stick together," Tanya shouted as she went back inside.

As we strolled by the library, Lena White, the librarian, offered a friendly wave while skillfully maneuvering a rack of books back inside from the sidewalk.

Finally, we arrived at Micky's Magical Things, the new store everyone had been talking about. The storefront was whimsical, with twinkling lights and a sign that seemed to shimmer in the sunlight.

"Micky's supposed to be able to talk to dead people," Jill whispered as we entered.

A tinkling bell welcomed us inside, like a secret invitation to an enchanting world. The store was filled with strange and wonderful objects—crystals, tarot cards, and curious artifacts. Micky, a friendly-looking man with a mysterious air, greeted us with a knowing smile.

"Welcome, Loretta and Jill. How can I assist you today?" he asked, his voice carrying a rich English accent.

I felt a shiver run down my spine. How did he know our names?

"We're just looking," Jill replied, giving me a tug towards her. "He knows us," she whispered in my ear.

My heart raced. Now I knew if anyone could help me escape Roy, it was Micky Vermooch. I wandered through the aisles, marveling at the strange and beautiful items. I desperately wanted to buy something magical that could change my life.

Suddenly, Gail, my neighbor, appeared from behind a shelf. "Loretta, Jill, you shouldn't be here alone. There's a serial killer on the loose. I'll drive you home."

My heart sank. My chance to find something magical had slipped away. As we turned to leave, Micky leaned in close to me and whispered, "Your mom wants you to know that everything will be okay. She asked me to tell you to give your teddy bear, Mr. Teddy, with the blue butterfly on his bum, an extra hug from her." He chuckled softly. "Remember, she's always with you."

I froze, and my eyes widened in shock. *How could he know about my mom? Or Mr. Teddy?*

"What's wrong with you," Gail grabbed my hand. "Why are you just standing there?"

"What did he tell you?" Jill muttered.

I looked up at Micky in awe. He gently patted me on my head and winked.

"You are really magical," I gasped.

"Magical," he chuckled. "I don't know if you would call me magical. I'm just an ole gypsy boy." He crouched down, bringing his face close to mine, and softly said, "Magic can be powerful, but it's not always what you expect. Sometimes, the real magic is finding the strength within yourself."

I smiled.

"Everything will soon be fine," he said in a whisper, his blue eyes twinkling.

"I'm sorry, Micky," Gail interrupted. "Loretta, I really need to go. Patricia and Margie are waiting for me."

Gail herded us towards her car. Before sliding into the back seat, I looked back at Micky's store, a mixture of emotions swirling within me.

As we drove out of town, I glanced out the window and spotted Roy's black truck parked outside Jason's Bar. My stomach churned with dread. On the ride home, I was lost in my thoughts, except for Jill's constant chattering to Gail and an occasional slap on my knee.

When we stopped at Jill's house, her mother was waiting outside.

"Where on earth have you been?" she shrieked as she opened the car door and leaned inside. "Thank you, Gail, for taking her home."

"No problem," Gail replied.

"I'll see you tomorrow, Loretta," Jill shouted as her mom closed the door.

"Is everything okay?" Gail asked. "You've sure been quiet since we left Micky's store."

"Yes, I'm fine."

Finally, we pulled up to my house. I thanked Gail as I rushed out of the car. Her two friends were already on the porch waiting for her. It was the same two as this morning. They stared at me as I hurried inside.

I went straight to my room, opened the window to let in the sweet sounds of the ocean breeze, and curled up in the center of my bed. The words Micky told me kept replaying in my head. I picked up Mr. Teddy, looked at the blue butterfly embroidered by his stubby tail, and then held him tightly against my chest as tears soaked my pillow.

"Mom said everything will be okay. We just have to believe it, Mr. Teddy. We just have to believe."

~ 5 ~

THE MONSTER!

The first light of dawn peeked through the thin curtains, which fluttered gently in the breeze, casting a soft, grayish light over my small room. I blinked sleepily and looked around, feeling a little confused. I glanced at the clock, my heart fluttering as I realized Roy hadn't come to wake me like he did every morning.

He must not have come home last night. I thought, a rare smile spreading across my face.

I hugged Mr. Teddy close, whispering into his plush ear, "Micky was right. Things are going to get better."

I got dressed quickly, feeling a burst of energy from the peaceful morning. After tucking Mr. Teddy safely under my pillow, I stepped out of my room, the wooden floorboards creaking under my feet.

As I walked down the hallway, I peeked into Roy's room. It was quiet and still, with his stuff scattered around as usual. I glanced into the kitchen and the living room, but Roy was nowhere to be found. I rushed to the back door and looked out to see if his truck was in the driveway. It wasn't.

"Yay," I shouted excitedly, twirling around in a circle. "I hope you never come home."

Outside, the early morning air was breezy and warm. On the porch, Gail and her two friends sat sipping coffee from mismatched mugs. Their laughter stopped suddenly when they saw me.

"Loretta, come here," Gail called out, her tone sharp.

I walked over, my stomach knotting with unease.

"These are my two best friends, Patricia Noack and Margie Richard," Gail said, gesturing towards them with a tight smile. "They've heard about Roy; apparently, he didn't come home last night."

How on earth did they know that? I wondered, swallowing hard.

"He was parading around town, drunk and loud, being obnoxious with his friend Gary," Patricia grumbled.

"He was probably too drunk and spent the night in the parking lot at Jason's Bar," I said quickly, hoping to avoid more questions.

"No," Gail shook her head. "We heard that he was hanging all over Mary Campbell and left with her."

"I don't know who that is, but he goes out with a lot of women," I shrugged, nervously tugging at my book bag.

"Does he make a habit of it?" Gail pressed, her gaze sharpening. "I get the drunk part, but does he frequently leave you alone like this?"

Not often enough, if you ask me.

Before I could answer, Margie added, "You know he can get into some serious trouble by doing that."

Panic bubbled inside me. "I'm... I'm late for school," I mumbled, turning and running before they could say anything else.

As I crossed the road, the Preacher called out to me, "Watch out for cars, Loretta!"

"Yes, sir," I replied, quickening my pace.

Why are they so worried about Roy? Who cares if he doesn't come home?

I turned back to see if Gail and her friends were still watching me, but they were busy talking to Preacher John.

I hurried down the street, spotting Jill and Tricia waiting in front of Jill's house. Tricia Grigar and her family moved here last year and instantly became friends with Jill and me. Mrs. Staggs calls us the three musketeers.

I ran up to them, panting. "Guess what? Roy didn't come home last night. Micky said things would get better!"

"Is that what he told you yesterday?" Jill asked.

"He told me that my mom wanted me to know that everything would be okay, and he knew about Mr. Teddy!" I grabbed Jill's hand. "You were right. He can talk to the dead."

"I told you so," Jill said smugly.

"Is that the new shop in town, Micky's Magical Things?" Tricia asked, her hazel eyes widening in surprise.

"Yes," I shook my head. "He even knew our names."

"That's probably because Gail was talking to him and told him before she came out from the back aisle," Jill chuckled.

"You're probably right," I giggled.

"Who is Mr. Teddy?" Tricia asked, nervously running her fingers in her short, light brown hair.

I looked at Jill, and we both started laughing.

"I want to go back to Micky's store today after school," I said, checking the side pocket of my book bag to make sure my money was still there.

"I can't go," Jill sighed. "My mom is picking me up today."

"I'll go with you," Tricia said eagerly.

"Okay," I grinned.

The school day dragged on, each class a blur of half-heard lessons and restless thoughts. I couldn't wait for the final bell. When it finally rang, I quickly gathered my things and met up with Tricia.

As we walked through the neighborhood, Tricia asked, "Why aren't we taking the walking path? Isn't this way longer?"

"We heard something in the woods," I said, lowering my voice to a whisper, "which was pretty spooky."

Tricia's eyes widened, and I could practically see her imagination running wild.

"That's why we're taking the main road," I added with a grin. "It only adds about ten minutes and is much safer."

She nodded in agreement, but I could tell the thought of the eerie woods lingered in her mind, just as it had in mine.

I also shared all the rumors I'd heard about Micky's Magical Things. She was just as excited as I was to check it out.

However, our mood shifted as we neared the Sheriff's office. We noticed a large, agitated crowd murmuring and shouting, demanding answers. The air was thick with tension and fear - another woman had gone missing. This was the fifth one.

We stood on our tiptoes, trying to see what was happening. The Sheriff stood on the steps, attempting to calm the crowd. "Everyone, please, go home. We're doing everything we can. I promise you. We will find Mary Campbell and the other four women."

Mary Campbell! That's who Gail and her friends said Roy was with!

A distressed woman was at the front, sobbing uncontrollably to the Mayor about her missing daughter.

Tricia tugged on my sleeve. "Let's go to Micky's," she suggested, but before we could move, Patricia Noack appeared.

"You two should get home," she said sternly. "It's not safe out here."

We didn't argue. We turned and headed back, the weight of the town's fear pressing down on us.

When I finally arrived home, my heart sank. Roy was sprawled on the couch, his clothes filthy and his face scratched up as if he'd been in a fight. I stood frozen in the doorway, the realization dawning on me like a cold, dark shadow.

Could he be the serial killer?

My breath caught in my throat. I quickly retreated to my room, my mind racing. I hugged Mr. Teddy tight, trying to quiet the storm of fear and confusion inside me. Micky had promised things would get better, but now I wasn't so sure.

As the house settled into an uneasy silence, I lay in my bed, eyes wide open. Every creak and groan of the old house sounded like a whisper of impending doom. The thought of Roy being the killer gnawed at me, refusing to let go. I remembered the scratches on his face, the wild look in his eyes when he was drunk, and the way he disappeared for hours without explanation. It all added up in a terrifying way, and the more I thought about it, the more certain I became that something was horribly wrong.

A sudden noise down the hall made me sit up straight. The sound of something heavy being dragged across the floor sent chills down my spine. I crept out of bed and peered down the hallway, my heart pounding in my ears.

At the end of the hallway, I saw Roy staggering and mumbling incoherently. His eyes were dark, almost hollow, as if haunted by something terrible. He turned towards me, and for a moment, our eyes met. My blood ran cold.

"Go back to bed," he slurred, his voice dripping with menace.

I didn't need to be told twice. I fled back to my room, shutting the door quietly but firmly. I climbed into bed, pulling the covers over my head, clutching Mr. Teddy like a lifeline.

Sleep was impossible. Every sound, every shadow seemed to whisper my darkest fears. I thought of the missing women, their faces from the posters flashing in my mind. Was Roy responsible? The thought was too terrifying to contemplate, but the evidence was mounting.

I need to find out the truth. For the sake of the missing women and my own safety, I needed to find out if the monster sleeping under my roof was also theirs—my stepdad.

~ 6 ~

WAKEY! WAKEY!

"Wakey! Wakey!" Roy's voice thundered through my bedroom door, jolting me awake from a nightmare about him.

I rubbed my eyes and squinted at the darkness outside my window. It was way too early.

"Get up and make me some eggs and toast," he barked. "And coffee!"

He looked awful, even worse than last night. His face was covered in scratches like he'd been in a fight with a cat, but we don't have a cat.

"Where did you get all those scratches, Roy?" I asked, trying to keep my voice steady even though my heart was pounding. His glare made me freeze.

"Mind your own business, Loretta," he snapped.

I knew better than to push it. When Roy got angry, it was like a storm was coming.

As I cooked his breakfast, I watched him pack a bag. He'd never left me alone before, but now he said he had some business out of town and wouldn't be back for two or three weeks. My stomach twisted. What kind of business? Why now?

When he finished eating, he grabbed his bag and walked out the door. I followed him, keeping a few steps back. His black Dodge pickup was in the driveway, looking as big and mean as always. But today, the back of it was covered with a tarp. My heart skipped a beat. What was he hiding under there? A body? The thought made my skin crawl.

I watched from the back porch as he threw his bag into the truck and started the engine. He didn't even look back at me. The truck roared to life, and he drove off down the road, disappearing into the morning fog.

The house felt eerily quiet and still, as if it were holding its breath, anticipating something bad. The shadows seemed longer, and the creaks and groans of the old floorboards echoed louder than usual. Every little noise made me jump—the fridge's hum, the clock's ticking, and the wind whispering secrets through the cracks in the windows. It was as if the house held a big secret and was too scared to reveal it.

It was Saturday, and I had the whole weekend to myself. I was free to do what I wanted for the first time but felt more trapped than ever. My heart felt heavy, and my thoughts were all jumbled. I couldn't stop thinking about Roy and his scary eyes, the way he looked worse than ever, and that tarp in the back of his truck.

I knew I needed to tell Jill about Roy. She was my best friend and always knew what to do. But the idea of saying it out loud made my stomach twist even more. What if she didn't believe me? What if Roy found out I told? I felt a lump in my throat as I thought about it.

Suddenly, I heard the rumble of Roy's truck in the driveway.

Why is he back? He must have forgotten something.

"Loretta," he shouted, poking his head inside the door. "I'm leaving my truck here, and Gary is going with me!"

"Yes, sir," I softly replied, walking towards the door.

"This is the first time I'm leaving you alone for this long," he said, a smirk playing on his lips. "I know I stay out all night, but never for days at a time. So, behave as if I'm still here, and remember, all the rules still apply. You may not see me, but I'll be watching you," he raised his eyebrows and narrowed his eyes. "You understand me?"

"Y..yes, sir," I nervously blurted.

He shook his head and chuckled, closing the door behind him. I waited, my heart pounding in my chest, straining to hear every sound. The slam of Gary's Charger door and the roar of the engine finally broke the tense silence. I hurried to the window, watching as they pulled out of the driveway. Only then did I bolt to my room, my footsteps echoing in the empty hallway, the fear pushing me faster as I sought the safety of my own space.

I quickly got dressed and rushed outside. As soon as I stepped out, I saw Gail sitting on her porch. I immediately looked away and hurried down the steps towards the road.

"I know you're not pretending you didn't see me sitting here, young lady," she shouted.

I stopped and glanced back at her with a sheepish smile.

"Get over here," she demanded. "I want to talk to you."

I slowly made my way to her house and plopped down in the hot pink chair. Gail looked at me with her usual curious eyes, studying me up and down.

"Ole Roy was up early this morning," she said, raising her left eyebrow and glaring at me over her cup of coffee.

"How did you know that?" I asked, surprised.

"Well, the whole neighborhood knows when he comes and goes," she chuckled. "His truck is loud enough to wake the dead."

I giggled.

"Did he act differently this morning?" she asked.

I can't tell her anything about the scratches on his face or him leaving town.

"Not really," I said, shrugging my shoulders.

"You know that Mary Campbell is missing, and the last person she was seen with was him?"

"I don't know anything," I quickly said, hoping she wouldn't press me further.

Gail studied me for a moment, then smiled.

"Is he going to be gone for a while?"

"Yes, most of the day," I replied. "Why?"

"Do you want to ride into town with me? I'm going to Catrina's Closet to buy a new bathing suit," she said with a grin.

"Can we go to Micky's Magical Things too?" I asked, eager to talk to Micky.

"Of course! It wouldn't be a trip to town without stopping there," she replied, her grin widening as she pulled out her car keys.

When we got to town, it was like stepping into a hive of buzzing bees. Everywhere we went, people were talking about the missing woman, Mary Campbell. Groups of neighbors huddled together on sidewalks, their voices low and filled with concern. Storekeepers chatted with customers, their eyes darting around as if they expected Mary to walk by at any moment.

The air was thick with nervous whispers and worried looks. I could hear snippets of conversations:

"Have you heard anything new?"

"I can't believe she's just gone."

"I heard that she was with Roy."

"What if something terrible happened?"

Everyone seemed on edge, glancing over their shoulders and clutching their bags a little tighter.

As we walked down the main street, even the usually cheerful shop windows seemed somber. Posters with Mary's picture were taped up everywhere, her smiling face looking out at us with a caption that read, "Have You Seen Me?" It made my stomach twist into knots.

"Isn't that a shame," Shannon sighed, taping the poster on the glass by her door. "I was just helping her the other day. She was making plans for her first cruise next year." Her voice trailed off, a mix of sorrow and disbelief hanging in the air as she stepped back to look at the missing person's poster, her eyes filled with worry.

Gail, noticing my unease, squeezed my hand gently. "Don't worry, sweetie," she said softly. "They'll find her."

I think I already did, this morning in the back of Roy's pickup truck.

"What's going on next to the bakery?" Gail asked.

"That's Brenda Menifee," Shannon replied, glancing over. "She's opening up a coffee shop, Bayou Bliss."

Brenda, a beautiful black woman with a radiant smile, was busy directing movers as they carried in furniture.

Gail nodded, a smile spreading across her face. "Bayou Bliss, huh? That sounds like it will be a wonderful addition to the town."

Shannon sighed, her expression turning serious. "Yeah, but after she hears about the serial killer, she'll probably change her mind."

"That's the truth," Gail muttered, reassuringly squeezing my hand. "Let's head to Catrina's Closet first, and then we can grab some lunch."

At Catrina's, Gail surprised me by buying the lavender dress I had been admiring with Jill the other day. I couldn't believe it—it was the prettiest dress I had ever seen. For a moment, all thoughts of Roy, the missing woman, and the nervous whispers vanished. Pure excitement and happiness filled me as I twirled in front of the mirror, the lovely fabric swirling around me.

"You look absolutely stunning in that dress," Catrina commented, her long brown hair pulled back in a ponytail and her brown eyes twinkling as she watched me. "It suits you perfectly."

I smiled at her, feeling a warm, happy feeling spread through me. "Thank you, Ms. Catrina. It's really beautiful."

Catrina nodded, her smile gentle. "Sometimes, a little bit of joy is all we need."

Gail chimed in, "She's right. You deserve it."

As we left the store, the lavender dress carefully wrapped and tucked under my arm, I felt a renewed sense of hope. I couldn't help but feel a little guilty for being happy while everyone else was so worried.

We went to Tanya's Crawfish Shack for lunch, and as always, my happiness was short-lived. Just as we placed our order, the Sheriff walked in. He spotted me right away and came over.

"Hey Loretta," his voice soft but serious. "Is Roy at home?"

"No," I said, my heart pounding. The Sheriff didn't say anything else, but his face showed he was worried.

"Do you want me to give him a message," Gail asked.

"No," he replied, smiling softly, gently tapping our table before walking away.

"What on earth did Roy do now," Gail grumbled.

He killed Mary Campbell. Why else would the Sheriff want to talk to him? I thought, the suspicion gnawing at me as I shrugged and took a sip of my iced tea.

"He probably wants to talk to him because everyone in town saw him all over Mary before she disappeared," she stated, rolling her eyes. "He's not the brightest crayon in the box."

The whole situation felt like a storm waiting to break, with tension thickening in the air, ready to unleash at any moment. It was only a matter of time before everything came crashing down.

After lunch, Gail and I walked over to Micky's Magical Things. Walking inside, we saw Mary Campbell's mother talking to Micky. She was crying, her voice choked with emotion.

"Micky, please, you have to help me find her," she sobbed, clutching his arm desperately. "I don't know what else to do."

Micky looked genuinely concerned, his brow furrowed as he tried to comfort her, his voice calm and soothing.

I watched from a distance, my heart aching with the need to talk to him, but he was clearly caught up in the moment with her.

Gail noticed my impatience and leaned in. "Looks like he's really tied up. What did you need to ask him about?" she asked softly, her eyes filled with understanding.

"It's nothing important," I replied, glancing back at Micky and Mrs. Campbell.

"That poor woman," she said, shaking her head. "I can't imagine what I would do if something ever happened to Stephanie."

"Who is that?" I asked.

"My daughter," she replied, smiling softly. "Thank goodness she's away in college."

Suddenly, Mary's mother let out a heart-wrenching scream. Micky quickly wrapped his arms around her, trying to calm her down.

"He must have told her some bad news," I whispered.

Gail gave me a sympathetic look. "Well, let's head home."

Even though I didn't talk to Micky, I should have felt happy. After all, I got the dress I was dreaming about, but all I could think about was Roy's scratched-up face, the tarp-covered truck, and Mary Campbell. I needed to talk to Jill. She'd know what to do.

As soon as we got home, I put the dress in my room and raced down the street to Jill's house, my heart pounding in my chest. I had to figure out what Roy was hiding, for the sake of the missing women and for my own safety.

When I knocked on Jill's door, a chill ran down my spine. The weekend had just begun, but I already knew it was going to be a long, scary one.

~ 7 ~

HIDDEN SECRETS

The heavy wooden door of Jill's house creaked open, and her mother, Mrs. Ecker, stood there with a welcoming smile. "Loretta, come on in, dear. Jill's in her room."

I stepped inside, feeling the warmth and safety of their home envelop me. The aroma of freshly baked cookies filled the air, a comforting contrast to the tension suffocating me at my own house.

I rushed upstairs to Jill's room and knocked softly. She opened the door, her blue eyes sparkling with curiosity. "Hey, Loretta! What's up?"

I took a deep breath, trying to steady my nerves. "We need to talk. It's important."

Jill's smile faded as she stepped aside to let me in. We sat on her bed, the pink bedspread crinkling beneath us. "What happened?" she asked, her voice low and concerned.

"Roy left early this morning," I began, my voice trembling. "He looked worse than ever, his face covered in scratches. He left town with Gary, saying he had business to take care of. They took Gary's Charger and left Roy's truck in the driveway, probably so people would think he's still home."

Jill's eyes widened as she listened, the gravity of the situation sinking in.

"I think he's involved in Mary Campbell's disappearance?"

"What?" she shrieked. "If Roy's involved in her disappearance, he's probably behind all of them."

I nodded slowly. "I'm not sure, but he's definitely hiding something. He had a tarp covering the bed of his truck. While Gail and I were having lunch at Tanya's, the Sheriff showed up and asked about Roy."

Jill's face turned serious. "We have to find out what he's up to. If he's involved, we need to tell someone."

"But how?" I asked, feeling a wave of helplessness wash over me.

Jill thought for a moment, her fingers tapping rhythmically on her knee. "We need to check his truck. If he's hiding something, it might be in there."

My heart raced at the thought. "But he's gone. How can we get into the truck? The tarp is strapped down tightly."

"We'll figure it out," Jill said determinedly. "Meet me at your house in an hour. I'll bring my dad's toolkit."

The hour crawled by slowly, my anxiety growing with each passing minute. Finally, I saw Jill approaching, a small toolbox in hand. We waited until the street was quiet and then crept towards the driveway.

The black Dodge pickup loomed ahead, the tarp still covering the back. My hands trembled as Jill handed me a screwdriver. "I'll keep watch. You try to lift the tarp."

Taking a deep breath, I nodded and approached the truck, Roy's ominous words echoing in my mind: "I'll be watching you." I quickly glanced around, feeling the weight of his threat. The straps holding the tarp were tightly secured, but I finally managed to loosen one and carefully peeled back the tarp.

A wave of horror washed over me as I saw what was beneath. There, hidden under the tarp, were blood-stained clothes and a large, dirty shovel. My stomach churned, and I had to fight back the urge to vomit.

"Jill," I whispered urgently, my voice trembling. "Look at this."

She hurried over, her eyes widening in shock as she saw the contents. "We need to take this to the Sheriff," she said, her voice firm. "This is evidence."

Just then, a sound behind us made us both jump. We turned to see Gail standing there, her eyes wide with disbelief. "What are you two doing?" she asked, her voice barely above a whisper. "Isn't Roy home?"

"No Gail, he's not here," I said, my voice breaking. "We think Roy is involved in Mary Campbell's disappearance. Look at this."

Gail's face paled as she saw the bloodstained clothes and shovel. She took a deep breath, trying to steady herself. "We need to go to the Sheriff. Now."

We quickly covered the truck back up and hurried towards town, the weight of our discovery pressing heavily on our shoulders. The streets were eerily quiet as we approached the Sheriff's office.

Inside, Sheriff Johnson was speaking with a deputy, his face grave. He looked up as we entered, his eyes narrowing with concern. "What's going on, girls?"

Jill stepped forward, her voice steady despite the fear in her eyes. "Sheriff, we found something in Roy's truck. You need to see it."

The Sheriff's expression turned serious as he listened to our story. He nodded, a hint of urgency in his movements, and grabbed his hat. "Show me," he said, his voice firm and authoritative.

We led him back to the house, the tension palpable in the air. As we uncovered the truck, our hearts sank. The bloody clothes and shovel were gone. In fact, the bed of the truck was clean and sparkling, as if someone had scrubbed it spotless.

"This can't be," I stammered, my voice barely a whisper. "It was here, I swear."

The Sheriff frowned, his eyes scanning the truck bed. "Are you sure, Loretta? There's nothing here."

Tears welled up in my eyes as I looked at Jill, my heart pounding with fear and frustration. "I'm sure, Sheriff. We both saw it."

Gail stepped forward, her face pale but resolute. "They're telling the truth, Sheriff. I saw it too."

The Sheriff sighed, rubbing the back of his neck, the weight of the situation evident in his posture. "Alright. I believe you," he said, his voice softer now. "But without any evidence, there's not much I can do right now."

His words hung in the air like a dark cloud, and a sense of helplessness settled over us. The truth was there, just out of reach, but it seemed to be slipping through our fingers.

He turned to me, worry written all over his face. "Loretta, if Roy comes back and you feel threatened, you come straight to me. Understand?"

I nodded, my mind reeling from the turn of events. The Sheriff's words were meant to comfort me but did little to quell the fear gnawing at my insides.

As we walked back to the house, Gail put a comforting arm around my shoulders. "We'll figure this out, Loretta. Don't worry," she said with a reassuring smile. "Is Roy coming home tonight?"

He's got to be nearby since he's the one who cleaned out the truck bed.

"Yes," I replied, trying to sound more braver than I felt.

"I better get home," Jill said, hugging me tightly. "Are you going to be okay?"

I nodded, giving her a small smile.

"Well, alright then. I'll see you tomorrow," Jill added, picking up the toolbox. "If you need anything, just call me."

"Okay, I will." I nervously glanced around, looking for any signs of Roy as Jill walked across the street.

"What are you looking for?" Gail asked. "Do you want to stay with me? You would be safe at my house. I don't feel right about you staying with him."

I could see the worry in her eyes, and it tugged at my heart. The thought of staying with Gail, where I'd be safe, was tempting, but I knew that Roy was out there—somewhere—watching me. The fear of what he might do if he found out I wasn't at home gnawed at me, and despite the safety Gail offered, I couldn't shake the feeling that staying away from him might only make things worse.

"No," I replied, dashing up the steps to my house. "I'll be fine."

Before Gail could say another word, I rushed inside and locked the door.

Roy had hidden the evidence, and now I was more afraid than ever. He was watching me, but why? The nightmare was far from over, and I had a sinking feeling it was only just beginning.

~ 8 ~

GLIMMER OF HOPE!

The sun was just beginning to rise, casting a soft, rosy hue over Bayou Vista. What happened last night was still stuck in my mind, but today, I was determined to have a normal day—well, normal for me, anyway. Jill, Tricia, and I had planned to go into town and make our usual stops. Maybe, just maybe, I'd find something at Micky's Magical Things to help me make sense of everything.

I met Jill and Tricia at the corner of the street. Jill's face lit up when she saw me. "Hey, Loretta! Ready for our adventure?"

I nodded, trying to muster a smile. "Yeah, let's go."

"What are you girls up to so early?" Preacher John called out from across the street as he wheeled his trashcan to the curb.

"Nothing much," I stammered. "Just heading into town."

"You girls be careful," he warned, giving us a stern look.

"We will," I assured him, nodding quickly. "Let's go before Gail and her friends come out."

As we hurried away, Jill nervously tugged at my hand. "I told Tricia about what we found in the bed of Roy's truck yesterday and how it vanished without a trace."

"What do you think happened to it?" Tricia asked, her eyes wide with concern.

"Well, I've been thinking about it all night," I said, turning to face them. "Do you think Roy is really gone, or could he be watching the house?"

"He has to be watching the house," Jill nervously muttered. "But why?"

"I don't know," I sighed. "But I'm sure I will find out."

The walk into town was filled with the usual chatter, but there was an underlying tension in the air. People were on edge about the missing women, and whispers followed us as we walked past groups of anxious townsfolk.

Our first stop was C&D Kwik Stop. As we entered, the familiar jingle of the doorbell greeted us. Dondi, with his ever-present friendly smile, waved us over. "Well, look who it is! My favorite trio. Here, have some candy." He handed each of us a piece of our favorite treat.

"Thanks, Mr. Dondi," we chorused, the sweetness of the candy momentarily lifting our spirits.

We continued down Main Street, passing familiar faces and shops until we reached the new coffee shop,

Bayou Bliss. Brenda stood outside, arranging some potted plants by the entrance. She looked up and greeted us with a warm smile. "Hello, girls. Come to check out the new place?"

"Yes, ma'am," Jill said, her curiosity shining through.

"Would you girls like a pastry?" she asked kindly.

"No, ma'am," Tricia replied, stuffing the rest of the candy bar into her mouth.

Her smile widened. "I'm Brenda Menifee. It's nice to meet you all. I hope you'll stop by for some hot chocolate or pastries sometime."

"Thank you, Ms. Brenda. Your place is beautiful," I said with a smile. "We'll definitely come by."

Our last stop was Micky's Magical Things. The shop looked even more magical today. The tinkling bell above the door welcomed us as we stepped inside. Micky was behind the counter, sorting through some crystals. His eyes lit up when he saw us.

"Ah, Loretta, Jill, Tricia! Welcome back," he said, his voice soothing and melodic. "What brings you here today?"

"How did he know my name?" Tricia whispered, grabbing me by my arm.

"He's magic," I whispered back, smiling.

I glanced around the shop, my eyes landing on a small, sparkling stone on a nearby shelf. "I was hoping you might have something... special."

Micky's expression turned thoughtful.

"Something that could help me...."

Before I could say another word, he reached for the stone I had been eyeing and handed it to me. "This is a wishing stone. It's said to make your deepest desires come true, but you must believe in its power."

I held the stone in my hand, feeling its smooth surface. "How do I use it?"

"Close your eyes, make your wish, and hold the stone tightly. Believe with all your heart, and the magic will work," Micky explained. "But you know, Loretta, if you believe in something strongly enough, it will come true. You don't really need a stone for that."

I nodded, clutching the stone. "Thank you, Micky, but right now, I think I need all the help I can get."

Before he could say anything more, curiosity got the better of me. "How did you know about my mother?"

Micky's eyes softened. "I've always had a gift, Loretta. I can sense things and see things others can't. Your mother's spirit is strong."

Just then, the doorbell tinkled again, and Sheriff Johnson walked in, followed by Mary Campbell's mother. Her eyes were red and swollen from crying. The atmosphere in the shop shifted, becoming heavy with tension.

"Evening, Sheriff," Micky greeted with a nod. "What brings you to my humble establishment?"

Sheriff Johnson removed his hat, running a hand through his graying hair. "Just looking for some answers, Micky. Seems we're in short supply these days."

Micky nodded, his expression serious. "Of course, Sheriff. What can I do?"

Mary Campbell's mother stepped forward, her voice trembling. "Please, Micky, can you find my daughter? You were right yesterday—Mary was wearing her ruby necklace."

Micky placed a comforting hand on her shoulder. "I'll do my best. Let's talk in the back."

"Loretta," Sheriff Johnson smiled. "I haven't forgotten you. I'm looking into what we talked about."

"Thank you," I replied.

As Micky and Mary's mom moved towards the back of the shop, Micky turned to us. "Take care, girls."

We nodded, feeling the seriousness of the moment. As we left the shop, I held the wishing stone tightly in my hand, feeling a tiny spark of hope in my life.

Walking back home, Jill gave me a reassuring hug. "You'll be okay, Loretta."

I nodded, grateful for her comfort.

With friends like Jill and Tricia by my side and the magic of the wishing stone, I felt a little less scared about what might come my way.

~ 9 ~

NIGHT OF NORMALCY

As we walked back from town, I couldn't shake the feeling of being watched. I looked around nervously.

"You feel that too?" Jill asked.

"Yes, someone is watching us," I replied, my voice trembling.

Suddenly, Gary, Roy's friend, appeared behind us. "What are you girls doing?" he asked.

"We're just coming back from town," I said, trying to sound calm.

"Well, you girls need to be careful," he said with a glare. Before I could ask him anything, he vanished as quickly as he had appeared.

"That's weird," Jill said, her eyes wide.

"Really weird," I agreed. "He's supposed to be working out of town with Roy."

As we turned the corner onto my street, I saw Gail sitting on her porch, looking right at me. She stood up when I got closer, and I could see she was really worried.

"Loretta, can we talk for a minute?" she called out, waving me over.

I nodded.

"We'll see you later," Jill said.

"Okay."

I watched Jill and Tricia cross the road as I made my way to Gail's house. When I reached her porch, she motioned for me to sit down on one of the hot pink chairs. "How was town?" she asked gently.

"It was okay," I replied, trying to sound casual. "We stopped by C&D Kwik Stop, visited Brenda Menifee's new coffee shop, and then went to Micky's."

Gail's eyes narrowed slightly. "Did you find anything?"

I hesitated, then decided to tell her the truth. "Micky gave me a wishing stone. He said it can make my deepest desires come true if I believe in it."

Gail raised an eyebrow. "Do you believe in his gift, Loretta?"

"Absolutely," I said without hesitation. "He knew things that no one else could have known."

Gail nodded thoughtfully. "That's quite something. But I also wanted to ask you about Roy. Where is he? Tell me the truth."

"He's out of town," I answered honestly. "He said he had business to take care of and wouldn't be back for a couple of weeks." Before I could mention anything about Gary, she erupted.

"Why didn't you tell me that?" she scolded, her voice laced with worry. "You shouldn't be alone in the house, especially not with Roy. It's really not safe for you to be by yourself. I worried about you all night last night. If something happens to you, I'll never forgive myself." The concern in her voice made it clear just how much she cared.

"I was scared to tell you," I muttered, lowering my head.

Gail's expression softened, and she placed a hand on my shoulder. "Why don't you stay with me, Loretta? I can order a pizza tonight, and you can sleep in my daughter Stephanie's old room. It'll be fun."

My heart lifted at the idea. The thought of spending a night away from the house, away from the memories and the fear, sounded like a dream. "Really? That would be great!"

"Of course," Gail said with a warm smile. "Go get your pajamas, and we'll have a nice, relaxing evening."

I ran back to my house, my feet barely touching the ground. Inside, I grabbed my pajamas and Mr. Teddy from under my pillow. I took one last look around my room, feeling a weight lift off my shoulders, then hurried back to Gail's.

When I returned, Gail was already on the phone, ordering pizza. "You like pepperoni, right?" she asked with a wink.

I nodded eagerly. "Yes, please!"

Gail smiled and finished the order, then led me inside. The warmth of her home wrapped around me like a comforting blanket. Stephanie's old room was cozy and inviting, with soft pastel colors and posters of musicians on the walls.

"Make yourself at home," Gail said, patting the bed. "I'll be right back with some blankets."

I sat down on the bed, hugging Mr. Teddy tightly. For the first time in as long as I could remember, I felt a sense of peace wash over me. Gail returned with a pile of blankets and a big, fluffy pillow.

"Here you go," she said, arranging the blankets. "The pizza should be here soon. In the meantime, why don't we watch a movie?"

We settled in the living room, the glow of the television casting a warm light around the room. Gail put on a family movie, and we laughed and talked, the tension of the past few days slowly melting away.

When the pizza arrived, we ate until we were stuffed, the cheesy, savory slices filling us with a comforting warmth. Gail told me stories about Stephanie when she was my age, making me laugh until my sides hurt.

Roy, his terrible treatment, the bloody clothes, and the missing women were never mentioned. I knew Gail was trying to help me forget about everything, at least for one night.

Later, as I lay in Stephanie's bed, the soft hum of the house lulling me to sleep, I realized it was the first time

I felt normal. The nightmares that usually haunted me seemed distant, kept at bay by the kindness and warmth of Gail's home.

I closed my eyes, clutching Mr. Teddy close, and whispered, "Thank you, Mom. I know that you sent Micky and Gail to help me. I believe."

A sense of warmth and comfort washed over me, as if her presence was still here, watching over me, guiding me through the darkness.

~ 10 ~

A MORNING OF COMFORT AND FEAR

Waking up at Gail's house felt like a dream. The soft, cozy bed, the gentle light filtering through the curtains, and the delicious smell of bacon wafting through the air—it was a world away from the cold, tense mornings at my own house. I stretched and yawned, feeling more rested than I ever had in my life. I got out of bed, hugged Mr. Teddy, and tucked the wishing stone into my pocket before heading to the kitchen.

I found Gail in the kitchen, humming softly as she cooked breakfast. "Good morning, sweetie," she said with a warm smile. "Did you sleep well?"

"Yes, ma'am," I replied, sitting down at the table. "Thank you for letting me stay here."

Gail set a plate of bacon and eggs in front of me. "You're always welcome here, Loretta," she said warmly. "I don't want you staying in that house alone, or with Roy. Honestly, I'd rather you never go back there, but I understand he's your guardian, even if he doesn't act like much of one. If Roy ever gets loud or abusive, or even if he looks at you funny, you come straight to me," she insisted, pushing the salt and pepper shakers toward me. "Do you understand?"

"Yes, ma'am."

"I got my own opinions formed about that murderous, abusive asshole," she muttered.

The bacon was crispy, the eggs perfectly scrambled, and I savored every bite. Gail joined me at the table with her coffee, and we chatted about our plans for the day. For a moment, everything felt normal, and I almost forgot about the darkness lurking in my life.

But as I walked to school, the weight of my worries returned. I met up with Jill and Tricia, and we headed to class together. The halls were buzzing with excitement about Halloween, which was just two weeks away. Mrs. Staggs had promised us a fun day of decorating and party planning.

In class, Mrs. Staggs greeted us with a big smile. "Good morning, everyone! Today, we're going to start planning our Halloween party. Who's excited?"

The room erupted in cheers and raised hands. Mrs. Staggs laughed and began assigning tasks. Some kids were in charge of decorations, others for games, and a few for snacks. Jill, Tricia, and I were put in charge of making spooky invitations.

As we worked, Mrs. Staggs' cheerful demeanor changed. "Before we get too carried away, I need to tell you all something important," she said, her voice serious. "There's been another missing woman in town. Patti Williams. Please be careful, and don't go anywhere alone. Stick together and look out for each other."

A heavy silence fell over the room. Patti Williams. Another woman was taken. Fear crept into my heart, and I glanced at Jill and Tricia, who looked just as scared as I felt.

Is that the reason Roy is away? Maybe he's taking the women to the old campground where he used to take me. There's nothing around for miles, just a giant mosquito-infested lake filled with alligators.

The rest of the day passed in a blur. The joy of Halloween planning was overshadowed by the news of the missing woman. When the final bell rang, I hurried back to Gail's house, eager to tell her what had happened.

Gail was in the kitchen, preparing dinner. She looked up as I walked in, her face lighting up. "How was school, Loretta?"

I took a deep breath. "There's been another missing woman. Patti Williams."

Gail's smile faded, replaced by a look of concern. "Oh, no. That's terrible. We need to be extra careful."

I could tell she was thinking about Roy by the way she looked at me.

She pulled me into a hug, and I felt a wave of comfort wash over me. "I'm making chicken nuggets and fries for dinner," she said, trying to lift my spirits. "Why don't you help me set the table?"

After dinner, Gail sat down with me to go over my homework. She was patient and kind, explaining everything in a way that finally made sense. It was the first time anyone had ever really helped me with schoolwork. Roy always had a saying: *You're the one in school, not me—so you figure it out.* But with Gail, it felt different, like someone actually cared whether I understood or not.

As I finished my last math problem, Gail went into the living room to turn off the TV, and I felt the wishing stone in my pocket. I pulled it out and held it tightly, closing my eyes.

"I wish Roy would never come home, and I could stay with Gail forever," I whispered, pouring all my fear and hope into the wish.

I opened my eyes, half expecting something to happen, but everything was the same.

Then I turned around and saw Gail standing at the kitchen door, smiling at me. "That's my wish too," she said softly.

"Really?"

"Yes, it sure is," she grinned. "Ready for bed?"

I nodded.

As I climbed into bed, I held Mr. Teddy close and whispered to him, "Maybe things will get better. Maybe this time, the magic will work."

Suddenly, a loud noise shattered the stillness of the night. I sat up, heart pounding. Gail rushed into the room, her face pale. "Stay here," she whispered urgently. "Lock the door behind me."

I did as she said, fear gripping me. I could hear Gail talking to Preacher John at the front door, her voice tense. After what felt like an eternity, she returned and knocked on the bedroom door. I quickly opened it.

"It was just the wind knocking over a trash can," she said, trying to sound calm. "Everything's fine."

But I could see the fear in her eyes. We both knew that the wind wasn't the only thing to be afraid of.

As I lay back down, clutching Mr. Teddy and the wishing stone, I couldn't shake the feeling that something terrible was about to happen.

~ 11 ~

THE TOWN MEETING

The next day, the whole school was abuzz with the news of a big town meeting in the evening. It was all the teachers could talk about. The news of Patti Williams' disappearance had shaken the whole town. Six women have disappeared in less than two months. People were on edge. Store owners, residents, everyone was planning to be there. Even though I wasn't sure what to expect, I knew I had to be there too.

By the time evening rolled around, the town square was packed with people, all gathered for the big meeting. The tension in the air was thick. The sun was setting, casting an eerie glow over the angry and fearful crowd.

"I'm going to sit up front," Gail said, her voice trembling slightly. "Do you girls want to go with me?"

"No, ma'am," I replied. "We'll stay back here."

"Okay," she nervously smiled, looking for her two friends, Margie and Patricia, in the crowd. She spots Patricia and waves. "You girls, meet me back at the car when this is over."

"Okay," we replied.

Jill, Tricia, and I found a spot near the back, where we could see everything but stay out of the main fray. The square was buzzing with nervous energy. I scanned the faces around us, recognizing many of the store owners: Shannon from Shanster Travels, Cindy and Dondi from C&D Kwik Stop, LaDonna from Frog's Delight, Tanya from the Crawfish Shack, Jason from Jason's Bar, Catrina from Catrina's Closet, and even the new lady, Brenda from Bayou Bliss. Lena, the librarian, was standing with our teacher, Mrs. Staggs, and our bus driver, Matilda. Nearly every resident of Bayou Vista was there, including the town's outcast, Rosie Fontenot.

Mayor Strittmatter, Judge Hopper, and Sheriff Johnson stood on a small stage, trying to address the crowd. The Mayor's voice boomed over the chatter. "Everyone, please settle down. We understand your fears and concerns. The Sheriff is working tirelessly to find these women."

The crowd erupted in shouts and questions:

"What are you doing to keep us safe?"

"Why haven't you found them yet?"

"What about our children?"

The voices were growing louder and angrier.

Sheriff Johnson raised his hands, trying to get everyone's attention. "Please, everyone, we're working around the clock. We have leads, and we're following up on them.

We need your help too. If you see anything suspicious, report it immediately."

A woman's voice cut through the noise, sharp and panicked. "Sheriff, is it true that Patti Williams was last seen at Jason's Bar?"

"Oh My God!" another lady shouted. "That's the last place Mary Campbell was seen too!"

"What are you doing about that?" Dondi yelled, his face red with fury.

"That place needs to be shut down!" Rosie shouted, a sly smirk playing on her lips.

The crowd surged forward, the fear and frustration almost tangible.

"My bar has nothing to do with the disappearances," Jason yelled.

"Look, folks, everyone needs to calm down," the Mayor shouted, but the growing uproar drowned out his voice.

"We've interviewed Jason Riesenbeck, the bar's owner, and the two incidents have nothing in common," the Sheriff pointed at Jason. "According to him, the two women left the bar alone."

"We heard Roy was with Mary Campbell!" Preacher John exclaimed, raising his voice above the rumbling crowd.

"Did you talk to Roy?" Catrina demanded, her voice sharp.

"No," the Sheriff replied. "We're unable to locate him."

"This is unacceptable!" shouted Tanya, her voice filled with rage. "My daughter walks home from school every day. How do I know she's safe?"

"We're scared, Sheriff!" Lena's voice cracked with emotion. "You have to do something!"

"Oh, for Pete's sake," Rosie yelled. "What the hell do you want them to do?"

"Find the bastard!" a man angrily shouted.

As the Sheriff tried to respond, the crowd's unrest grew. People were shouting over each other, demanding answers, demanding action. It was chaos.

I noticed Micky standing off to the side, watching the crowd. Our eyes met, and he gave me a reassuring nod, as if to say he was keeping an eye on things. It made me feel a bit better knowing he was there.

Then, something really strange happened. While the Mayor was still talking, a man suddenly grabbed Micky and dragged him away from the crowd. I nudged Jill and whispered, "Did you see that?"

Jill followed my gaze. "No, what happened?"

"Some man just grabbed Micky," I whispered urgently. "Should we go over there and see what's happening?"

"No, it was probably the father of one of the missing women," Jill replied. "I'm sure Micky's alright."

"Yeah, you're probably right," I said, trying to shake off the unease.

The meeting continued, with more questions and very few answers. People were angry and scared, demanding more action from the Sheriff and the Mayor. As the crowd began to disperse, the tension was still palpable. Everyone was on edge, unsure of what would happen next.

As we were leaving the square, Jill, Tricia, and I talked about what we had heard. "Do you think the Sheriff will find the missing women?" Tricia asked, her voice filled with worry.

"I hope so," Jill replied. "But it's going to take more than just the Sheriff."

I nodded, watching Micky and the man from earlier as they stood in front of his shop.

"What do you think Loretta?" Tricia asked.

"I think it's going to take Micky to solve this one."

Suddenly, I heard someone call out my name—it sounded like Roy. I turned quickly around, but no one was there. When we got to Gail's car, I heard it again. My stomach clenched, and I froze.

"What's wrong, honey?" Gail asked.

"Someone was shouting my name," I replied, my voice trembling.

"I didn't hear anyone," Gail said, putting a comforting arm around me. "It was probably someone from school."

"Yeah, maybe," I muttered. But deep down, I couldn't shake the feeling that the voice I'd heard really sounded like Roy.

"Loretta, just remember, I'll always be here for you."

I leaned into Gail, feeling some of the tension melt away.

Tricia and Jill joined the hug, saying, "We're here too."

On the ride home, I glanced up at the sky. The first stars were starting to twinkle, and the night air was cool and refreshing. I took a deep breath, feeling the wishing stone in my pocket. I didn't know what was going to happen next, but I had friends who cared about me, and thanks to Micky, I had a little bit of magic. And for now, that was enough.

~ 12 ~

SOMEONE IS WATCHING!

The following day, the whole school was talking about the disappearances and the growing fear gripping Bayou Vista. Walking through the crowded hallways, I couldn't shake the feeling that someone was watching me. But every time I turned around, there was no one there.

"Hey, Loretta!" Jill called out, catching up to me by the lockers. "What happened to you?" She laughed, gently running her fingers through my messy hair. "Did you get any sleep last night?"

"Not much," I admitted. "I kept having those nightmares again." I grabbed my notebook from out of the locker. "Last night, when we were at Gail's car, I thought I heard Roy shouting my name."

Jill frowned, her eyes filled with concern. "We need to find out where Roy is. We can't just wait around for something bad to happen."

"I know," I said. "But what can we do?"

Jill glanced around to make sure no one was listening. "Meet me after school. Tricia's mom is picking her up today, but we can head into town and see if we can learn anything from Micky."

I nodded.

The day dragged on, with everyone on edge. Mrs. Staggs tried to keep us focused, but it was impossible to ignore the tension in the air. Every little noise made me jump, and I kept looking over my shoulder, convinced that someone was watching me.

After school, Jill and I snuck off to town again. The streets seemed quieter than usual, with fewer people out and about. Everyone was scared, and it showed. As we approached the town square, we saw Micky talking to a couple of customers outside his shop. He saw us and gave a small nod, but his expression was serious.

"We need to talk to him," Jill whispered. "He has to know something."

"Hey, Mr. Micky," I said, trying to sound casual. "Do you have a minute?"

Micky glanced around before motioning us inside. "Come in, girls. Let's talk."

Once we were inside, Micky shut the door and lowered his voice. "I've been keeping an eye on things, and I think I know where Roy is hiding. But it's dangerous. You need to be careful."

"Where is he?" Jill asked, her eyes wide.

"There's an old abandoned factory on the outskirts of town," Micky said. "I've seen him there a few times. I don't know what he's doing, but it's not good."

"Should we tell the Sheriff?" I asked, my heart pounding.

Micky nodded. "No, I called and left him a message to contact me."

Jill and I exchanged nervous glances.

"I feel like someone is watching me," my voice cracked. "Is it Roy?"

"Yes," Micky replied. "So be very careful where you go and who you talk to. Not everyone is who they seem."

As we left the shop, I felt a shiver run down my spine. The sense of being watched was stronger than ever.

"I feel like we should tell the Sheriff, too, but how can we tell him if Roy is watching you?" Jill asked.

"We can't," I replied, my voice trembling.

"Loretta," Jill gasped. "I wonder how long he's been watching you?"

"All my life," I sighed.

When I got home, Gail was waiting for me. "Where have you been?" she asked, her voice full of worry.

"I was with Jill," I said. "We had to talk to the Micky about something important."

Gail's face softened. "Just be careful, Loretta. I don't want anything to happen to you."

"I will," I promised, feeling the weight of the wishing stone in my pocket. "I'll be careful."

That night was long and filled with restless dreams. In one, I was running through the darkened streets, chased by shadows that whispered my name. In another, Roy stood at the foot of my bed, his face twisted with anger.

Early the next morning, I heard a noise outside. My heart pounded as I crept to the window and peeked out. In the dim morning light, I saw a figure standing at the edge of the yard, watching the house.

I froze, my heart racing. Who was it? Was it Roy? I squinted, trying to see more clearly, but the figure slipped into the bushes and vanished. With a shaky breath, I collapsed back onto the bed, my heart still pounding in my chest.

~ 13 ~

THE SHERIFF'S VISIT

After I calmed down, I got dressed and went into the kitchen.

"Good morning, honey," Gail said, handing me a breakfast sandwich. "Did you sleep okay?"

"Yes," I lied.

"I have an appointment in Pelican Bay today, so I'll take you to school and pick you up afterward," she said, sipping her coffee.

As Gail drove me to school, we saw police cars patrolling the streets, their lights flashing ominously.

"Well," Gail grumbled. "It's about time you see the police out here."

Someone probably reported seeing Roy this morning.

When we arrived, she gave me a tight hug. "Be careful, Loretta. Remember, stick with your friends."

"I will," I promised.

At school, the atmosphere was somber. Mrs. Staggs tried to keep our spirits up with Halloween decorations and activities, but it was clear that everyone was on edge. Jill, Tricia, and I worked on our spooky invitations, but our hearts weren't in it.

During lunch, we gathered in a quiet corner of the cafeteria, and I told Jill and Tricia about my nightmares.

"I feel like someone is watching me all the time," I said.

"Who?" Tricia asked, her voice trembling.

"Early this morning, I saw someone staring at Gail's house. It looked like Roy," I replied, glancing around nervously.

"Did you tell Gail?" Jill asked, her face serious.

"No," I admitted. "I wasn't sure if she would believe me."

"We believe you," Tricia said firmly.

As the day went on, I just knew something big was about to happen.

When the final bell rang, I hurried to the front of the school and felt a wave of relief when I saw Gail waiting for me. We drove home in silence, both lost in our thoughts.

I was helping Gail in the kitchen that evening when we heard a loud knock at the door. The sudden noise made me jump, and I could see Gail tense up, her face turning pale. She wiped her hands on a towel, moving slowly like she was preparing for bad news.

"Stay here," she whispered to me before heading to the door.

I watched her open it, and there stood Sheriff Johnson, his big frame filling the doorway and casting a long shadow into the dim hallway. His face was serious, and his eyes looked heavy with worry.

"Evening, Gail. Loretta," he said, nodding at me. "Did Roy come home yet?"

Gail shook her head, her voice steady but quiet. "No, Sheriff. He left town a few days ago and hasn't come back. I'm looking after Loretta while he's gone."

The Sheriff's eyes narrowed, and I saw the lines on his forehead deepen. "Do you know where he went?"

Gail glanced at me, her face hard to read. Then she turned back to the Sheriff. "He didn't say. Just that he had some business to take care of."

Sheriff Johnson looked at me, and his stern face softened when he saw how scared I was. "Loretta, do you know where Roy might have gone? Did he say anything to you?"

"He told me he was going to be gone for a couple of weeks for work, but someone told me they saw him at the old abandoned factory on the outskirts of town," I said, feeling a lump in my throat that I tried to swallow down. "He left with Gary. I thought they were working together out of town, but I saw Gary the other day, so I guess he just dropped him off."

The Sheriff's face got even more serious. "I saw Gary earlier today. He didn't mention anything about Roy. I'm going to have another talk with him."

"Is something wrong, Sheriff?" Gail asked, her voice shaky, her hand gripping the doorframe.

The Sheriff sighed, and it sounded like it was heavy with frustration. "We're trying to figure out what's going on with these disappearances. Roy's name has come up a few times, and I need to find him."

Gail's face paled, and she leaned closer to the Sheriff, lowering her voice. "Do you think he's involved?"

"We don't know yet," the Sheriff said, his jaw tight. "But we need to talk to him." He looked at me, "Thanks for telling me about the factory, Loretta. We'll check it out."

After the Sheriff left, Gail shut the door and turned to me, her eyes full of worry. She took a deep breath as if she were getting ready to say something important. "Loretta, if there's anything you're not telling me, you need to say it now. It's important."

I swallowed hard, feeling the pressure of her gaze, the weight of the truth pressing down on me like a boulder. "I...I don't know anything else, Gail. I promise."

She nodded slowly, but I could see the worry in her eyes. "Alright, sweetie. Let's finish up dinner and try to relax."

The rest of the evening was quiet and tense. We ate dinner, but it didn't taste like anything, and the only sound was the clinking of our silverware. Gail kept looking at me, and I could tell she was worried about more than just Roy's whereabouts.

After dinner, I went to my room and sat on the bed, holding my wishing stone tightly. I felt so scared, and the shadows in my room seemed to grow darker, making everything feel more frightening. Every creak of the house made me jump, and I imagined Roy sneaking back, angrier than ever.

I closed my eyes and whispered to the stone, "Please keep everyone safe. Please make sure Roy doesn't come back."

I lay in bed, clutching the stone, and my mind was full of scary thoughts. What if Roy did come back? What if he found out I'd talked to the Sheriff? The fear made it hard to breathe.

I tried to find comfort in the house's familiar sounds—the refrigerator's hum, the distant barking of a dog, the soft sound of the ocean through the window. But every noise seemed louder, and every shadow looked like a monster. I hugged Mr. Teddy tightly, wishing I could hide under the blankets forever.

Hours went by, and I couldn't sleep. Every time I closed my eyes, I had the same nightmares. Just when I fell asleep, I heard a noise that made my heart race—the sound of a car engine and a door slamming. I froze, my heart pounding in my chest. Was Roy back? I listened hard, every muscle in my body tense.

I heard voices coming from the front yard of my house. Slowly, I crept to the window and peeked out, my breath catching in my throat. Sheriff Johnson was back, and he wasn't alone. Two deputies stood with him, their flashlights cutting through the early morning gloom. They were talking to someone, but I couldn't see who it was. I leaned out the window, trying to hear what they were saying.

The Sheriff's voice was firm. "We need to know where Roy is. Now."

A muffled reply, followed by more urgent questions. My mind raced, trying to figure out what was happening. Were they getting closer to finding him? Or was this another dead end? Who were they talking to?

Finally, the voices moved away, and I heard the car doors slam shut. The engine roared to life, and they drove off into the morning light. I collapsed back onto the bed, my heart still racing. The Sheriff was determined to find Roy, and I had to believe he would.

As I lay there, the shadows slowly disappearing with the dawn, I held the wishing stone tightly and whispered one last wish. "Please, keep us safe. Please, let the Sheriff find Roy before it's too late."

~ 14 ~

THE MISSING CAR

As soon as I walked out of my room, I could feel that something was wrong. Gail was already up, sitting at the kitchen table with a worried look on her face.

She looked up as I walked in, and I could tell something was wrong. "Loretta," she said, her voice shaking slightly, "I talked to the Sheriff this morning. They found Patti Williams' car at the abandoned factory."

My heart skipped a beat. "Did they find her?" I asked, my voice barely above a whisper.

Gail shook her head. "No, honey. Not yet. But the Sheriff wanted me to tell you to be extra careful. He said you and your friends shouldn't go anywhere alone."

I nodded, feeling a knot of fear tighten in my stomach. "Okay, Gail. I'll be careful."

"Honey, who told you about the abandoned factory?" she asked, curiosity filling her eyes.

"Micky," I replied. "He was planning on telling the sheriff himself."

Gail gave me a tight hug. "I'll take you to school every day and pick you up afterward. And remember, no sneaking off into town unless I'm with you."

I nodded again, feeling the weight of her worry pressing down on me. "Yes, ma'am."

At school, the atmosphere was even more tense than usual. It was as if the air itself was charged with fear and worry, and everyone seemed to be walking on eggshells. Everyone was talking about Patti Williams and the abandoned factory. Whispers filled the hallways, and nervous glances were exchanged between students and teachers alike. Mrs. Staggs tried her best to keep us focused on our work, but it was clear that everyone's mind was elsewhere.

During lunch, Jill, Tricia, and I found a quiet corner to sit in. "What do you think about the Sheriff finding Patti Williams' car?" Tricia asked, her eyes wide with fear.

"It's scary," I replied, glancing around to make sure no one was listening. "Gail told me this morning."

Jill nodded, her face serious. "The Sheriff called my mom and told her we shouldn't go anywhere alone. He knows we're always sneaking off to town."

"I know," I said, feeling a chill run down my spine. "Gail's taking me to school and picking me up from now on."

"Do they think that Roy is involved?" Tricia asked.

"The sheriff didn't say it outright, but I can tell that's what he's thinking," I replied, my voice shaky. "And I'm certain he is."

The rest of the day zoomed by in a blur. When the final bell rang, I felt like I'd been holding my breath all day. I grabbed my backpack and bolted to the front of the school. My heart raced as I scanned the crowd of parents and kids, searching for Gail. Finally, I spotted her by the curb, smiling at me. I let out a big sigh of relief and ran over to her, feeling a little bit safer now that she was here.

After school, Gail took me to Tanya's Crawfish Shack for dinner. As soon as we walked in, the yummy smell of seafood hit me, making my stomach growl. Tanya greeted us with a warm smile as we walked in.

"Hey there, sweeties," Tanya said. "How are y'all holding up?"

"We're doing okay," Gail replied, giving Tanya a small smile. "Just trying to stay safe."

Tanya nodded, her expression turning serious. "I heard about Patti Williams. It's just awful. Y'all be careful now, you hear?"

"We will," I said, trying to sound brave. "Thank you, Ms. Tanya."

As we ate, I couldn't help but notice how the town was starting to prepare for Halloween. Shanster Travels and C&D Kwik Stop were already putting up decorations, trying to bring some cheer to the town despite the fear that hung over it. Pumpkins, cobwebs, and spooky decorations adorned the storefronts, and for a moment, it felt like things might get better.

As Gail and I were leaving Tanya's, we noticed Rosie Fontenot picking up her food. She stood out with her wild, untamed hair and mismatched clothes, her face always set in a permanent scowl. Gail nudged me and whispered, "Bless her heart; Rosie always looks like she just rolled out of bed. But you know, she means well. She hasn't been the same since her husband's accident. It left her mean and bitter."

Rosie caught sight of us and gave a slight nod. "Evening, Gail. Loretta," she said, her voice gruff but not unfriendly.

"Evening, Rosie," Gail replied, her tone polite but distant.

As we walked back to the car, I couldn't shake the feeling that someone was watching us. The weight of the wishing stone in my pocket was a constant reminder of the danger that still lurked. When we got to the car, Gail noticed my nervous glances around. "What's wrong, sweetie?"

"I just feel like someone's watching us," I admitted, my voice trembling.

Gail's face turned serious. "Don't worry, Loretta. You're safe with me."

I wanted to believe her, but the unease wouldn't go away. As we drove home, I kept looking out the window, half expecting to see Roy following us.

That night, Gail made us hot chocolate, and we sat in the living room, trying to distract ourselves with a movie. But I could tell she was worried too. Her eyes kept darting to the window, and she jumped at every little noise.

"Do you think the Sheriff will find Roy?" I asked, my voice small.

Gail sighed, putting her arm around me. "I hope so, sweetie. He's doing everything he can."

We both jumped when we heard a knock on the door. Gail got up slowly, motioning for me to stay put. She opened the door to reveal Sheriff Johnson, looking even more serious than before.

"Evening, Gail. Loretta," he greeted us with a nod. "May I come in?"

Gail stepped aside, and the Sheriff entered.

"What's going on, Sheriff?" Gail asked.

"We talked to Gary," Sheriff Johnson began, his voice grim. "He claims he hasn't seen Roy in days. Loretta, are you sure it was Gary who picked him up that morning?"

I felt a cold shiver run down my spine. "Yes, Sheriff. I'm sure. It was Gary's car."

The Sheriff nodded, his brow furrowed. "Have you been back inside your house since then?"

I shook my head, my heart pounding. "No, I've been too scared."

"We need to get more of Loretta's things," Gail added, her voice trembling. "But we're too scared to go in there by ourselves."

Sheriff Johnson's expression softened. "Alright, let's go next door. I'll come with you."

We walked out into the damp night, the air thick with tension. As we approached my house, the familiar structure loomed in the darkness, every shadow seeming more sinister than usual. The creaking of the old wooden porch beneath our weight sounded like ominous whispers in the still night.

Sheriff Johnson took out his flashlight and shone it around the porch, the beam cutting through the darkness.

"Stay close," he instructed.

The front door creaked open, and the flashlight's beam revealed the inside of the house. Everything was just as I had left it, but the silence felt heavy. We stepped inside, and the Sheriff's flashlight illuminated the hallway.

"Where are your things, Loretta?" the Sheriff asked.

"In my room," I whispered, pointing down the dark hallway.

Gail and I followed closely behind the Sheriff, his flashlight our only source of light. Every creak of the floorboards and rustle of the curtains made my heart race. As we entered my room, I quickly grabbed my clothes, stuffing them into a bag.

"Is there anything else you need?" the Sheriff asked, his eyes scanning the room.

I shook my head, clutching my bag tightly. "No, that's it."

"Alright, let's get out of here," he said, turning to lead us back down the hallway.

"Does everything look the same as you left it?" he asked.

"Yes, sir," I nervously replied.

Just as we were about to leave, a loud thud echoed through the house. We all froze, and my heart felt like it was about to leap out of my chest. The Sheriff motioned for us to stay put and slowly made his way towards the source of the noise, his flashlight cutting through the darkness.

"Who's there?" the Sheriff called out, his voice firm and commanding.

The silence that followed was deafening. We held our breath, straining to hear any sign of movement. After what felt like an eternity, the Sheriff returned, his expression tense.

"There's no one here," he said.

Suddenly, we heard footsteps pounding down the hallway, followed by the back door slamming open. My heart stopped as a shadowy figure darted out of the house and disappeared into the night.

"Let's go! Now!" the sheriff grabbed my hand, pulling me close behind him and hurrying out of the house.

As we rushed back to Gail's house, a nagging sense lingered that someone had been watching us from the shadows.

When we got inside, Gail locked the door behind us, her hands shaking. "Are you alright, Loretta?"

I nodded, though my heart was still pounding. "I'm okay. Just scared."

The Sheriff gave me a reassuring smile. "You're safe now. We'll find Roy, and we'll make sure he doesn't hurt anyone else."

I nodded, clutching the wishing stone in my pocket. "Thank you, Sheriff."

"Keep your doors locked. I'll have one of my deputies keep an eye on your house, and we'll be patrolling the neighborhood looking for him," he said with a firm nod before walking out the door.

As I lay in bed that night, the events of the day replayed in my mind like a scary movie. The shadows in my room seemed to dance with a life of their own, and every creak of the house made me jump. Clutching Mr. Teddy tightly, I curled up under the covers, the wishing stone warm in my hand. With my heart full of hope and fear, I whispered a silent prayer for its magic to keep us safe. Eventually, exhaustion took over, and I drifted into a restless sleep, still holding on to my small beacon of hope.

~ 15 ~

SPIRITS AND GUARDIANS!

The next morning, I woke up feeling uneasy. Gail was already up, sipping her coffee at the kitchen table, her eyes tired and worried.

"Good morning, Loretta," Gail said, trying to sound cheerful.

"Morning," I replied, forcing a smile. "Did you sleep at all?"

"A little," she admitted. "How about you?"

"Not much," I said, thinking about the shadowy figure that had darted out of my house. "Do you think the Sheriff will find anything?"

"I hope so," Gail replied. "He's doing everything he can."

As we sat down to breakfast, the phone rang. Gail answered it, her face growing more serious with each word. "Thank you, Sheriff. We'll be there soon," she said before hanging up.

"What's going on?" I asked, my heart pounding.

"The Sheriff wants us to come to the station," Gail said, her voice trembling slightly. "He found something."

"I wonder what it was?"

"I don't know," she sighed. "I guess you'll have to miss school today."

"That's okay," I shrugged my shoulders. "To tell you the truth, I didn't feel like going anyway."

We quickly got ready and drove to the Sheriff's station. The tension in the car was unmistakable. When we arrived, Sheriff Johnson greeted us, his expression grave.

"Morning, Gail. Loretta," he said, nodding at us. "Thank you for coming."

"What did you find, Sheriff?" Gail asked, her voice steady but anxious.

"We searched the abandoned factory last night," he began, leading us to his office. "We found some evidence that might help us find Roy and Patti."

My heart raced as we entered his office. On the desk were several items: a torn piece of cloth, a set of keys, and a small notebook.

"This notebook was hidden in a corner of the factory," the Sheriff said, opening it to reveal scribbled notes and drawings. "Does this look like Roy's handwriting?"

I leaned closer, trying to make sense of the notes. They were filled with ramblings about the disappearances, cryptic messages, and strange symbols. One page had a detailed map of the town, with several locations marked.

"Yes, that's definitely his handwriting. He always makes his s's look like lightning bolts. What do these markings mean?" I asked, pointing to the map.

"We're not sure yet," the Sheriff replied. "But we believe these could be locations Roy frequented or places he intended to visit. We need to investigate each one thoroughly."

I quickly studied the map, trying to memorize each location before the sheriff put the book away.

Gail's face was pale. "Is there any sign of Patti?"

The Sheriff shook his head. "Not yet. But we're following every lead."

As we left the station, Gail turned to me, her voice firm but gentle. "Loretta, you're not going back to school until I've spoken with Mrs. Staggs about what's going on with Roy. It's just too dangerous right now."

I started to protest, but the look in her eyes told me she wasn't going to budge. "Okay, Gail," I said quietly.

"I need to stop by the library," Gail said. "I have a couple of books to return. With everything that's happening right now, who has time to read?"

As we drove past Micky's store, I noticed Micky standing on the sidewalk, talking to Mary Campbell's mom. I waved, and he waved back.

"That poor woman," Gail sighed. "My heart breaks every time I see her. She's at Micky's every day, begging for answers."

Gail and I made our way to the library, the one place in town that always felt like a sanctuary to me. As we entered, the familiar scent of old books and polished wood welcomed us. The library was quiet, only the soft hum of the air conditioning breaking the silence.

Lena White, Terrie Lawson, and Amanda Sheppard were busy at the front desk, their heads bent over various tasks. Lena looked up and smiled as we approached.

"Morning, Gail. Loretta," she greeted us warmly. "What brings you here today?"

"I need to return some books," Gail replied, holding up a small stack. "With everything that's going on, I haven't had much time to read."

Lena nodded, taking the books from her. "I understand. It's been a tense time for everyone."

As Gail handled her returns, I wandered through the aisles, feeling a strange sense of calm among the shelves. I loved the library, its rows of books offering an escape from the real world.

But today, something felt different. As I walked towards the back, I noticed Rosie Fontenot. Rosie is a deeply bitter and spiteful person, her heart filled with resentment. People say her bitterness stems from a tragic event twenty years ago when a plant explosion near Alligator Island left her husband blinded. Rosie was the only one still living in that area since the accident, and she came to the library almost every day, always sitting in the same spot with a notebook, researching the areas around Bayou Vista.

Gail joined me, and we both watched Rosie from a distance. She was hunched over her notebook, scribbling furiously, her eyes darting around as if she expected someone to snatch her secrets away.

"That's strange," Gail whispered, her brow furrowing. "What could she be researching so obsessively?"

Before I could answer, Lena approached us, her expression serious. "Rosie's been researching places near Alligator Island and other abandoned places around Bayou Vista," she said quietly. "It's like she's looking for something specific but never says what."

Gail's eyes widened. "That is strange. Do you have any idea what she's after?"

Lena shook her head. "I've asked her a few times, but she just smiles and says she's working on a project. I can't help but feel there's more to it."

As we stood there, Rosie looked up, her eyes meeting mine. For a moment, I saw something in her gaze that sent a chill down my spine—pure malevolence. She quickly looked away, returning to her notebook, but the image of her eyes stayed with me.

We approached Rosie cautiously. Gail cleared her throat softly, and Rosie looked up again, her eyes wary.

"Rosie, do you mind if we sit with you for a moment?" Gail asked gently.

Rosie glanced at her notebook, then back at us. "I suppose not," she said, her voice barely above a whisper.

We sat down across from her, and for a moment, no one spoke. Finally, Gail broke the silence. "We've noticed you've been researching the areas around Bayou Vista. Is there something specific you're looking for?"

Rosie's eyes flickered with uncertainty. "I'm just... curious," she said evasively. "There's a lot of history in this town."

"Yes, there is," Gail murmured softly.

Rosie's hands trembled slightly as she closed her notebook. "To tell you the truth, I've been looking into the old stories, the legends. There's something...something dark about this place," she whispered.

A chill ran down my spine. "What do you mean?"

Rosie looked around nervously, as if checking to make sure no one else was listening. "There are tales, stories about the land around Alligator Island. They say it's cursed, that the explosion twenty years ago wasn't an accident."

Gail and I exchanged a shocked glance. "Cursed? By what?" Gail asked.

Rosie leaned in closer, her voice barely above a whisper. "There's talk of an ancient spirit, a guardian of the swamp. Some say it's been awakened, and it's angry."

"What?" Gail shrieked.

"That's why it's only been women going missing," Rosie continued. "The guardian is supposedly searching for a virgin bride. Personally, I think it needs to find a different hunting ground besides Jason's Bar if that's what it's after."

Gail and I exchanged uneasy glances.

"That's why I've been researching," Rosie added. "I'm trying to figure out another way to appease it, to stop whatever is happening."

The air in the library seemed to grow colder as she spoke. "Do you really think this spirit is behind the disappearances?" I asked, my heart pounding.

"I don't know," Rosie admitted. "But if it is, we're all in danger."

Suddenly, the library's lights flickered, and our eyes widened with fear.

"What was that?" I shrieked.

"Fools," Rosie scoffed, bursting into laughter. "I was just messing with you. It's none of your damn business what I'm researching." She quickly gathered her things and hurried out of the library, leaving Gail and me sitting in stunned silence.

Lena came over, her face pale. "What did she say?"

Gail shook her head slowly. "She's out of her mind."

"She mentioned something about a spirit, a guardian of the swamp," I started.

Gail quickly interrupted, "Don't believe a word she said. She's completely unhinged."

"That's the truth," Lena agreed.

As we left the library, Gail turned to me and suggested, "How about we head over to Micky's?"

"Oh, yes," I replied eagerly.

As we stepped inside, a bell tinkled softly, and the smell of incense filled the air.

"Welcome!" Micky's voice called from behind the counter. "Loretta, Gail, it's so good to see you both."

"Hi, Micky," I replied with a smile.

Micky grinned. "Feel free to look around. If you need any help, just let me know."

As Gail wandered off to browse the shelves, I headed straight for a corner filled with old books. I ran my fingers over the spines, reading the titles: "Secrets of the Swamp," "The Witch's Grimoire," "Spells and Enchantments for Beginners." Each book seemed to promise a world of magic and mystery.

"Find anything interesting?" Micky asked, appearing beside me.

"I don't know," I admitted. "I was hoping to find something... special. Something that could help us."

Micky's eyes twinkled. "Magic can't solve all our problems, Loretta. But sometimes, it can help us find the strength we need to face them."

I nodded, feeling a little disappointed. "I just want to keep us safe."

He placed a hand on my shoulder. "You are. You're stronger than you think. And you have people who care about you."

Just then, the front door burst open, and Gary, Roy's friend, stumbled in, looking furious. Right behind him was Jason, the owner of Jason's Bar, following closely with a look of steely determination.

"Gary, calm down," Jason said, trying to reason with him.

"Don't you tell me to calm down!" Gary roared, turning to face him. "You're spreading lies about Roy!"

"They're not lies," Jason replied, his voice steady. "I know what I saw. Roy's involved in this somehow."

"You don't know anything!" Gary shouted, swinging a wild punch at Jason. "Roy's a good man!"

Jason ducked, and the punch missed, hitting a display of glass figurines instead. The sound of shattering glass filled the store, and Gail rushed over to pull me back as the fight escalated.

"Stop it! Both of you!" Micky shouted, trying to intervene. "This isn't helping anyone!"

But Gary was beyond reasoning. He swung again, this time connecting with Jason's jaw. Jason staggered back, but quickly regained his footing, tackling Gary to the ground. The two men wrestled, knocking over shelves and sending items crashing to the floor.

"Gary! Jason! Enough!" Micky yelled, but the men were too consumed by their rage to listen.

Suddenly, Gary managed to pin Jason down, his hands around his throat. "You take that back," he hissed. "You take it back, or I'll—"

Jason struggled, gasping for breath. "Roy... is... behind... it..."

With a roar, Gary tightened his grip, but before he could do any more damage, Sheriff Johnson burst through the door, followed by two deputies.

"Break it up!" the Sheriff commanded, pulling Gary off Jason. The deputies quickly restrained both men, and the store fell silent except for the sound of heavy breathing.

"What in the world is going on here?" the Sheriff demanded, looking from Gary to Jason.

"He's spreading lies about Roy," Gary spat, struggling against the deputies' hold.

"I'm telling the truth," Jason insisted, his voice hoarse. "I saw Roy near the factory the night Patti disappeared. He's involved."

The Sheriff's face darkened. "We'll sort this out at the station. Both of you, come with me."

As the deputies led Gary and Jason away, Micky turned to us, his expression troubled. "I'm so sorry about that. Are you two okay?"

"We're fine," Gail said, still holding my hand tightly. "But what Jason said... do you think it's true?"

Micky sighed. "I don't know, but I saw him at the factory multiple times with my own eyes."

The rest of our visit to Micky's was subdued. Gail and I helped Micky clean up the mess, working in silence.

As we left the store, an uneasy feeling crept over me, and I couldn't shake the sensation that we were being watched.

"What's wrong?" Gail asked, noticing my discomfort.

"Nothing," I replied, glancing around nervously.

Next, we went to Bayou Bliss Coffee House to wait for the town meeting to start. Brenda made me the best drink I'd ever had—a double chocolate chip frappuccino.

Later, we attended the town meeting at the community center. The atmosphere was tense, and everyone was on edge. I scanned the room for Micky, but he wasn't there. The main topic of discussion was whether or not to proceed with the Halloween festivities.

"Given the recent events, should we cancel Halloween this year?" The Mayor asked, looking around the room.

Voices murmured, some in favor of canceling and others arguing that the children needed some semblance of normalcy.

"I think we should go ahead with Halloween," Ms. Catrina said, her voice firm. "The children need something to look forward to. Maybe it will cheer everyone up."

After much deliberation, the decision was made to proceed with the Halloween festivities, though with extra precautions. There would be additional patrols, and parents were urged to accompany their children at all times.

As the meeting concluded, a lingering sense of unease settled over me, reminding me that despite our efforts to carry on as usual, the danger remained very real and present.

As we drove home, Gail squeezed my hand reassuringly. "We'll get through this, Loretta. We just have to be careful and stick together."

Back at home, Gail tried to distract me with a movie, but my mind kept drifting back to the fight. Jason's words echoed in my head: "Roy is behind it." Could it really be true? And if he was, what did that mean for me?

That night, I couldn't sleep. I lay in bed, clutching the wishing stone, desperately hoping for answers. It felt like the shadows were closing in on me, and I didn't know who to trust.

~ 16 ~

IT'S GONE!

The morning sun did little to lift the heavy feeling of dread that hung in the air. When we woke up, Roy's truck was gone. Gail looked really worried and called the sheriff right away. I could hear her voice shaking a little as she talked.

"Roy's truck is gone. He must have been hiding in the house again," she said, pacing the kitchen.

The sheriff's response made her face tighten even more. Gail's knuckles whitened as she gripped the phone.

"Alright, Sheriff. We'll be careful. Please let us know if you hear anything," Gail replied before ending the call.

She turned to me, her eyes serious. "There's another missing woman, Cathy Vedder," she said with a sigh. "I'm taking you to school. It's safer there than here."

As we drove, the silence was heavy, broken only by the hum of the car engine. When we arrived, Gail insisted on walking me to the office. The hallway felt unusually long, and everyone was staring at us.

In the office, we found Mrs. Staggs. She smiled at us. "Good morning, Gail. Is everything alright?"

"Morning, Melissa," Gail said, her voice a bit shaky. "I need to talk to you about something important."

Mrs. Staggs immediately became serious. "Of course, Gail. What's going on?"

"It's about Roy. He's gone missing, and we just found out there's another woman missing too. Cathy Vedder. I want to make sure you know, so you can keep a close watch on her," Gail explained, gesturing to me.

Mrs. Staggs came around the desk and put a hand on Gail's shoulder. "We'll keep a very close eye on her, Gail. You have my word."

Gail nodded, visibly relieved, and hugged me tightly before leaving. "Be careful, okay?" she whispered in my ear.

"I will," I promised.

As I walked to my first class, Jill and Tricia found me. "What's going on?" Jill asked, her eyes wide.

"Yeah, you look like you've seen a ghost," Tricia added.

I looked around to make sure no one else was listening and then told them everything. Their faces showed they were scared too, but it felt better having my friends know what was happening.

"We need to be careful," Jill said, her voice steady. "We'll stick together."

"Agreed," Tricia said, nodding. "No one goes anywhere alone."

After school, Gail was waiting for us. The ride into town was tense, the usual chatter replaced by a solemn silence. Gail parked in front of Bayou Bliss, where Patricia and Margie were already seated, their expressions mirroring the worry on Gail's face.

"Can we go to Micky's," I asked Gail.

"Sure, but stay there until I come to get you," she replied. She then followed us outside and watched us until we safely reached Micky's down the block.

Micky looked up as we entered, his friendly smile fading when he saw our expressions. "What's going on?" he asked, coming around the counter to meet us.

"Roy is still missing," I said, my voice breaking. "And there's another woman, Cathy Vedder. The sheriff told Gail this morning."

Micky's face darkened with concern.

"Also, his truck is gone, and we think he's been hiding in the house," I added.

"Your mom wants you to be extra careful," Micky said softly. "Stay by Gail's side. Don't wander off."

"I will," I promised, feeling a bit reassured by Micky's concern. "Can my mom hear me?"

"Of course she can, honey," he smiled gently. "Every word."

"Why can't I remember when she died?" I asked, my voice cracking.

Micky hesitated, then replied nervously, "Sometimes our minds block out the bad things."

"Did she die tragically?" I pressed.

"Let's not dwell on something we can't change," he said, swallowing hard and glancing around. "Now, where on earth did I put my coffee cup?"

I knew from his reaction what the answer was.

He tried to lighten the mood by asking about our Halloween plans. Jill and Tricia chimed in, talking about their costumes, and for a moment, the tension eased as we laughed and joked.

Gail eventually came to get us, and we all headed to Tanya's Crawfish Shack for dinner. The spicy, comforting food helped lift our spirits. The familiar hustle and bustle of the restaurant was a welcome distraction.

After dinner, Gail made calls to Jill's and Tricia's moms to ask if they could spend the night. To our surprise, they agreed. It was the first time any of my friends had spent the night with me.

As we walked back to the car, Jill leaned in close, her voice barely a breath above the wind. "Are we really safe at your place? I can't stop thinking... what if Roy's hiding just next door, watching every move we make?"

I glanced at Gail, who was walking a few steps ahead, her posture tense but determined. "I think so," I whispered back, trying to convince myself as much as Jill. "Gail won't let anything happen to us."

But even as I said it, I could see the way Gail's eyes darted to every shadow, how her hand hovered near her purse as if ready for something—or someone.

We spent the evening watching movies in the living room, trying to drown out the creeping unease with laughter and popcorn. It felt good to be with my friends, to share a few carefree moments despite everything hanging over us. But as I glanced at Jill and Tricia, a shadow crossed my mind—something Roy used to say, with that twisted grin of his: *"The more friends you have, the more trouble you're inviting."* I shivered at the memory, his words clinging like a cold fog.

Gail eventually dozed off in the recliner, her soft snores filling the room with a sense of security.

Around midnight, a noise outside snapped us out of our sleepy haze. We all bolted upright, fear tightening in our chests. Gail was instantly alert, snatching up a flashlight.

"Stay here," she whispered, already heading toward the door.

We huddled together, barely breathing, our hearts racing in sync with the seconds that dragged on. After what felt like forever, Gail reappeared, her face serious but calm, like she'd rehearsed it.

"Just a raccoon," she said, forcing a smile that didn't quite reach her eyes. "Go back to sleep."

We nodded like we believed her, but I could see it—the tightness in her grip on the flashlight, the way she didn't meet our eyes. It wasn't a raccoon. She knew it, and I knew it too.

I tried to convince myself everything was fine, but sleep didn't come easy after that. The fear lingered, pressing down on all of us, even as we pretended to settle back into our blankets. Still, being surrounded by my friends and having Gail close by made it a little easier to push those thoughts away—for now.

~ 17 ~

TICK TOCK!

The following day, Gail was already up, talking softly on the phone in the kitchen. I could tell by her tone that it was serious. As I shuffled into the kitchen, Gail quickly ended the call and turned to me with a forced smile.

"Good morning, sweetie. How did you sleep?"

"Okay," I lied. The truth was, I had spent most of the night staring at the ceiling, my mind racing with worries about Roy and the supposed raccoon. Gail had tried to sound convincing, but the way she gripped that flashlight like a lifeline told me everything I needed to know.

Jill and Tricia emerged from the living room, rubbing their eyes. "What's for breakfast?" Jill asked, trying to sound cheerful.

"I was thinking pancakes," Gail said, her smile becoming more genuine. "How does that sound?"

"Sounds great!" Tricia replied, her enthusiasm lifting the mood a bit.

As Gail cooked, the smell of pancakes filled the house. We sat around the table, chatting and laughing, trying to forget the shadows looming over us. After breakfast, Gail called Jill's and Tricia's moms to ask if they could spend the whole weekend with us. To our surprise and excitement, they agreed!

"Really? We can stay all weekend?" Jill asked, her eyes wide with delight.

"Yes," Gail said, smiling warmly. "I thought it would be nice for you girls to have some fun together."

Later that morning, Gail took us shopping for our Halloween costumes in the next town over, Pelican Bay. The little costume shop was packed with spooky decorations—cobwebs draped across the ceiling, glowing jack-o'-lanterns flickering in every corner, and eerie music playing softly in the background. We spent hours sifting through racks of costumes, trying on everything from princesses to vampires to mummies, our laughter echoing through the store as we struck silly poses in front of the mirrors.

"I'm going to be a witch," Jill announced, holding up a black dress and a pointy hat.

"I'm going to be a pirate," Tricia said proudly, holding up a tattered coat and a hat with a feather. She grinned, showing off the plastic sword she'd found to complete the look. To top it off, she even grabbed a stuffed parrot to perch on her shoulder, giving a dramatic "Arrr!" that made us all burst into laughter.

"I think I'll be a ghost," I decided, picking out a flowing white sheet with eye holes.

Gail smiled as she watched us, but I could tell she was still on edge. As we left the store and walked to the car, she kept glancing over her shoulder, her eyes scanning the street.

"Is everything okay?" I asked, noticing her tense expression.

"I just feel like someone might be following us," she said quietly. "Let's get to the car quickly."

We hurried to the car, drove back to Bayou Vista, and stopped at C&D Kwik Stop, where Patricia and Margie were waiting. Dondi and Cindy, the owners, greeted us warmly as we walked in.

"Hey, Gail! How are you holding up?" Dondi asked, his face full of concern.

Gail sighed. "It's been tough. Roy's still missing, and now there's another woman, Cathy Vedder, who's gone too."

Cindy came around the counter and gave Gail a hug. "We're here for you, Gail. Anything you need."

Dondi handed each of us a candy bar, trying to lift our spirits. "Here you go, girls. A little something to cheer you up."

"Thanks, Mr. Dondi," we said in unison, our smiles returning.

As Gail, Patricia, and Margie discussed the situation, we sat at a table near the window, munching on our candy bars and watching the world go by. Despite the seemingly ordinary scene, the unsettling feeling of being watched still lingered.

"Girls," Gail called out, as she waited for Patricia and Margie, who were standing in line to check out. "We're going to meet Shannon and LaDonna at Brenda's shop. Do you want to join us, or would you prefer to go to Micky's?"

"Micky's!" we chorused.

"Okay, but stay there until I come to get you," Gail replied firmly. She watched us walk down the block until we safely reached Micky's.

When we entered Micky's store, he greeted us with a warm smile. "Hey there! My favorite girls are back again today?"

"Hi, Micky!" we chorused.

I glanced around the store, feeling a bit more at ease. The shelves were lined with all sorts of fascinating new items—crystals, Halloween trinkets, and candles. We wandered through the aisles, chatting and picking up various items to examine, captivated by the intriguing array of treasures.

"Have you heard anything new about Roy?" I finally whispered to Micky, unable to keep the question inside any longer.

Micky's eyes darkened as he glanced around, making sure no one was listening. Leaning in closer, he lowered his voice. "Not much, but people are talking. Some say Roy's still around, hiding in plain sight. Others think he's long gone."

His gaze locked with mine, sending a chill down my spine.

"But I wouldn't trust those rumors. If Roy's still out there, and if he's really involved in any of this, he's not done yet. And we both know he's good at staying out of sight until he's ready to strike." Micky's voice was low and measured, each word laced with the kind of fear you only get from knowing someone like Roy all too well.

"That's true," I murmured, trying to push away the unease gnawing at me.

"Honestly," Micky continued, his voice tinged with frustration, "I'm starting to doubt that Roy's really behind all of this. He's no saint and definitely deserves to be behind bars, but something's not adding up. I talked to Mary Campbell's mom yesterday, and there was something off in the way she talked about the night Mary went missing. It might be nothing, but I told the sheriff. He's looking into it. Just promise me you'll stay safe, okay?"

I nodded, but Micky's words hung heavy in the air, making the fear I'd been trying to suppress bubble back up.

Sensing the tension, Micky tried to shift the mood, grabbing a box of new Halloween decorations he had just gotten in. "What do you think of these?" he asked, holding up a spooky skeleton with glowing red eyes.

"Those are awesome!" Jill exclaimed, her eyes lighting up with excitement.

We spent the next hour helping Micky set up his Halloween display, draping cobwebs and arranging creepy figures. Laughter filled the room as we joked about the silliest costumes and got caught up in the fun. For a little while, the fear that had been clawing at me faded.

Just as we finished, Gail walked in, looking a bit more relaxed. "Ready to go, girls?" she asked.

We nodded and said goodbye to Micky, though what he said about Roy earlier still clung to the edges of my thoughts. As we stepped outside, Gail turned to us, her tone clipped but calm. "I need to stop by the sheriff's office. You girls can wait in the car."

We exchanged glances but didn't argue, following Gail to the car. I couldn't help but notice the way she kept subtly checking over her shoulder as we walked, her guard up and her steps just a bit quicker than usual. It was a small thing, but it made the unease in my stomach twist even tighter. If Gail was this on edge, it meant that I wasn't the only one feeling Roy's shadow everywhere we went.

We piled into the backseat, and Gail drove us in silence. When we reached the sheriff's office, she parked and left the engine running, rolling the windows down just enough to let in the breeze. "I won't be long," she said before heading inside.

We watched quietly as people came and went, some with worried expressions, others looking frustrated. The tension in the air was thick.

"Do you think they'll find Roy?" Tricia asked softly, her voice barely above a whisper.

"I hope so," I replied, trying to sound confident but feeling a knot tighten in my stomach.

We sat there for what felt like forever, the minutes dragging by like hours. Finally, Gail emerged from the building, her expression unreadable. She slid into the driver's seat and sighed. "The sheriff says they're doing everything they can," she told us, but a heaviness in her voice made it hard to believe.

The rest of the day flew by as we made our way to Berry's Bayou Market, the brand-new grocery store owned by Mike and Kathy Berry. Gail picked up supplies for dinner while we wandered through the aisles. Jill and Tricia kept the mood light, cracking jokes and chatting about school.

In the bakery, Stefanie Jordan—nicknamed Firecracker for good reason—offered us warm chocolate chip cookies fresh from the oven. Just as Stefanie set the tray of cookies on the counter, Laurrie McBride, one of the cashiers, distracted her with small talk.

Meanwhile, Taylor McCray, the other cashier, dashed by, snatched the tray, and bolted toward the front. Stefanie's eyes widened before she took off after her, leaving us laughing so hard our voices echoed through the store. Gail smiled at our antics, but I could tell something was still weighing on her mind.

That evening, after dinner, we sat in the living room, the TV playing softly in the background. Gail looked at us and said, "I know things have been tough lately, but we're going to get through this. Just remember to stick together and be careful."

We nodded, feeling a bit reassured by her words. As the night wore on, we decided to watch another movie. Gail settled into the recliner, keeping a watchful eye on us as we sprawled out on the couch.

Halfway through the movie, a sudden knock at the door made us all jump, our hearts racing. Gail stood up, motioning for us to stay put. She walked cautiously to the door and peeked through the peephole.

"Who is that?" she whispered, though her voice barely reached above a breath. She crept away from the door and cautiously moved to the window, peering out into the shadows. "Where did he go?" she murmured to herself.

After a moment of hesitation, she unlocked the door and opened it just wide enough to reach down and pick up the package left on the porch. With a lingering glance outside, she quickly shut the door and brought the package inside, setting it on the coffee table.

"What's that?" Jill asked, her voice trembling as she eyed the mysterious package.

"I don't know," Gail replied, her brow furrowed as she noticed the absence of a return address. Carefully, she untied the string and lifted the lid, revealing a small, intricately carved wooden box. Inside was a folded note.

Gail's hands shook slightly as she unfolded the paper. She started to read aloud, but her voice faltered, and her face went ghostly pale. Without a word, she quickly crumpled the note and shoved it back into the box. The air in the room grew heavy and cold, as if all warmth had been sucked out.

"Alright, girls. It's time for bed," she said, her voice strained and trembling just enough for us to notice.

We didn't protest; the unease that had settled over us made it impossible to argue. As we got ready for bed, the creeping fear that had been lurking in the back of our minds resurfaced with a vengeance. The cozy living room suddenly felt vast and shadowed. We huddled together on the floor, wrapped in blankets, trying to draw comfort from each other's presence.

Gail sat in the recliner, her eyes constantly scanning the room, every creak and rustle keeping her on edge. After what felt like hours, Gail's eyes finally grew heavy, and she drifted into an uneasy sleep. Her steady breathing was the only sound in the room, but even that did little to calm the dread gnawing at me.

Curiosity tugged at me, relentless and insistent. I couldn't stand it anymore. I carefully slipped out from under my blanket and tiptoed over to the coffee table, making sure not to wake anyone. My heart pounded in my chest as I reached for the box, my hands trembling. Slowly, I lifted the lid and carefully unraveled the crumpled note inside.

My breath caught in my throat as I read the words scrawled in jagged, angry letters: *TICK TOCK!*

A wave of cold dread washed over me, and I quickly shoved the note back into the box, snapping it shut. My mind raced with questions—who sent this? What did it mean? But deep down, I knew it was a warning, a chilling reminder that time was running out.

I crawled back to my spot on the floor, my heart still racing. The room felt darker, the shadows thicker, as if they were closing in. Every creak in the house made me flinch, and the silence felt suffocating.

Eventually, exhaustion overtook me, and I drifted into a restless sleep, but it was anything but peaceful. My dreams twisted into a series of dark, shadowy corridors, each one echoing with the haunting words *'TICK TOCK.'* The sound grew louder and more menacing with every passing second, pounding in my head like a relentless drum. I tried to run, but the ticking followed, closing in on me, filling the darkness with a terrifying urgency I couldn't escape.

Even in sleep, the fear clung to me, wrapping itself around my thoughts like a cold, inescapable grip. When I finally jolted awake, drenched in sweat, the echoes of that eerie *'TICK TOCK'* still reverberated in my ears, making it impossible to tell where the nightmare ended and reality began.

~ 18 ~

INTO THE SHADOWS

The next morning, a sense of urgency buzzed in the air. Gail was up early, already dressed and looking more determined than ever.

"Morning, girls," Gail greeted us as we shuffled into the kitchen, my eyes still heavy from a restless night. Her tone was warm, but there was an edge of urgency in her voice. "I need to see the sheriff and show him the box that was left on the porch. I'm taking you girls to Micky's," she continued, her voice firm and leaving no room for debate. "He'll keep you safe."

We nodded, the unease from last night still hanging over us. After a quick breakfast, Gail drove us to Micky's store. The streets felt quieter than usual, and so did I. I couldn't stop thinking about that weird box and the eerie words, *'TICK TOCK.'*

"Remember to stay here until I come to get you," Gail said firmly before leaving us with Micky. Her eyes were sharp, filled with worry, making it clear she meant business.

Micky greeted us with his usual warm smile, but I caught the flicker of concern in his eyes. "Hey there, girls," he said, trying to keep his tone light. "How about we set up some more Halloween decorations today? I just got in some new spooky stuff."

We agreed, grateful for the distraction. As we rummaged through boxes of spooky decorations, Micky tried to lift our spirits with funny stories about past Halloweens—like the time someone swapped his store's candy with Brussels sprouts or when a prankster dressed as a ghost scared half the town. It helped a little, and we laughed, but the tension from last night still clung to me like cobwebs, never fully letting go.

After a while, I couldn't hold it in any longer. "Micky," I said hesitantly, biting my lip. "Can I talk to you alone?"

"Of course, honey," he replied, his cheerful smile quickly fading into a worried expression. "What's wrong?"

I took a deep breath, glancing around to make sure Jill and Tricia were busy in the back of the store. Lowering my voice, I leaned in. "Last night, we got a box delivered, and inside there was a piece of paper with the words *'TICK TOCK'* written on it. Gail doesn't know that I snuck a look."

Micky's face went pale, his usual calm demeanor replaced with concern. *"TICK TOCK,"* he muttered under his breath, almost as if he was trying to piece something together. He glanced toward the front door as if expecting someone to walk in at any moment. "This isn't just some prank, is it?" he asked, more to himself than to me.

"No," I whispered, my voice trembling. "It felt like a warning, Micky. Like someone's counting down to something bad."

He nodded, his expression grim. "You did the right thing telling me. We'll keep this between us for now. But listen to me, if anything else strange happens, you tell me right away. Understand?"

"I promise," I said, feeling a bit better now that I had shared the secret. "Thanks, Micky. Can my mom hear me?"

His expression softened, and he smiled gently. "Of course she can, honey. She's always listening, especially when you need her the most."

His words brought a warmth to my chest, easing the chill that had been there since last night. "Now," Micky continued, "let's finish up with these decorations and try to enjoy the day, okay?"

"Okay," I agreed, feeling a little lighter. As we returned to the boxes, the creepy note still lingered at the edge of my thoughts, but Micky's concern and reassurance made me feel a bit safer.

Around midday, a loud knock on the back door startled us. Micky went to answer it, and we peered around the corner to see who it was. Standing there was a tall man I didn't recognize, wearing a dark coat that seemed too heavy for the mild weather.

"Micky, we need to talk," the man said, his voice low and serious.

Micky glanced back at us and then stepped outside with the man, closing the door behind him. We huddled together, straining to hear what they were saying, but their voices were too muffled.

"What do you think they're talking about?" Jill whispered, her eyes wide.

"Maybe it's about Roy," Tricia suggested, her voice trembling.

A few minutes later, Micky came back inside, his face grim. "Girls, I need you to stay in the back room for a little while. I'll be right back."

We did as he asked, retreating to the back room and closing the door behind us. The minutes dragged by, each one feeling like an eternity. We tried to distract ourselves by looking through old books and trinkets, but it was hard to focus.

Finally, Micky returned, his expression softening when he saw our worried faces. "Everything's alright," he said, though his tone didn't quite match his words. "Why don't we take a break and have some lunch?"

We followed him to the small kitchen area, where he set out sandwiches and drinks. As we ate, Micky kept glancing at the door, as if expecting someone to burst in at any moment.

"I wonder what's taking Gail so long at the Sheriff's office?" I asked, feeling worried.

"Maybe they had a lot to discuss," Micky replied.

Just as we were finishing lunch, the door opened, and the Sheriff and Gail walked in. Gail was looking more stressed than I'd ever seen her.

"We need your help, Micky," the sheriff replied, his tone urgent. "There's something you need to see at the old mill."

Micky nodded, his face serious. "What's going on?"

The sheriff began explaining, "We have some new leads. Someone left me an anonymous note the other day, and when we followed up, we found Cathy Vedder's car abandoned near the old mill. Unfortunately, there was no sign of her."

We'd always been warned to stay away from the old mill, a crumbling relic of the past shrouded in rumors and ghost stories. The thought of it made my skin crawl.

"Are we going there?" Tricia asked, her voice small.

"Yes," Sheriff Johnson replied. "I need to show Gail, and it's important Loretta stays with someone at all times."

We piled into the sheriff's car, the atmosphere tense. Micky and Gail sat up front with the sheriff, while Tricia, Jill, and I squeezed together in the back, our nerves buzzing.

As soon as we pulled away from the curb, we started whispering to each other, our voices hushed as if speaking too loudly might summon whatever dark thing was lurking out there. "What do you think happened at the old mill?" Jill asked, her eyes wide with fear.

"Maybe it's haunted," Tricia suggested, trying to inject some humor into the situation, but her shaky voice gave away her own fear.

I barely heard them, my thoughts spiraling as I stared out the window at the passing trees. The old mill had always been a place of whispered legends and bad dreams—a place you dared each other to go near but never actually wanted to. I clutched my hands together, trying to steady myself as the car rumbled on, heading toward the one place I never wanted to face.

When we arrived, the sight of the old mill sent a chill down my spine. The fog had lifted, but the mill still looked menacing, its dark silhouette looming against the gray sky like a shadow from the past that refused to fade. The broken windows gaped like empty eyes, and the sagging roof seemed ready to collapse under the weight of old secrets.

As we stepped inside, the musty smell of decay and dust hit us, thick and cloying. The floorboards creaked under our feet, each groan echoing through the empty space as if the building itself was protesting our presence. Cobwebs clung to every corner, and the pale light filtering through the cracked windows cast eerie shadows that danced across the walls.

It was like stepping into a forgotten nightmare. The air felt charged with something dark and unseen, as though every horrible rumor we'd ever heard about this place might be waiting in the shadows, ready to come to life.

"We found this hidden panel last night," the sheriff said, pointing to a spot on the floor. He pried it open, revealing a narrow staircase leading down into darkness.

The sheriff grabbed a flashlight and led the way, the beam cutting through the darkness. The stairs creaked under our weight, and I couldn't shake the feeling that we were descending into the heart of the mystery.

"Micky," the sheriff asked, "while talking to any of the parents of the missing women, did you ever picture this place?"

"No," Micky replied, shaking his head.

At the bottom of the stairs, we found a small room. The walls were lined with shelves filled with old, crumbling books and dusty jars whose contents were long forgotten.

In the center of the room stood a large, wooden table covered in scattered papers and strange, unidentifiable objects—worn trinkets, pieces of metal, and what looked like hand-drawn maps. Everything was coated in a layer of dust, as if this room had been frozen in time, waiting for someone to uncover its secrets.

The beam of the sheriff's flashlight trembled slightly as we took in the scene, every detail adding to the overwhelming sense that we'd stumbled onto something we weren't supposed to see.

"What is this?" Micky asked, his voice barely above a whisper, the unease in the room thickening with every second.

"It looks like some kind of workshop," the sheriff replied, picking up an old book and blowing off a thick layer of dust. He flipped through a few pages, his brow furrowing. "Whoever was here was researching the area—digging into something."

As he spoke, my eyes scanned the wall, and my heart skipped a beat when I saw the photos tacked up. Among them were familiar faces—women from Bayou Vista who had gone missing. My breath caught in my throat as I spotted Roy's picture, his face circled in red ink, like a target.

"What does it mean?" I asked, my voice trembling.

"It's a timeline," the sheriff replied grimly, his eyes narrowing as he studied the wall. "Dates, names... someone's been tracking these disappearances."

Gail stepped closer, her face etched with confusion and fear. "Why would Roy's picture be up there if he's the one behind all of this?" she asked, her voice strained as she tried to make sense of it all.

The sheriff didn't answer right away. He stared at the wall, deep in thought. "Maybe it's not that simple," he said finally. "If Roy's picture is circled like this, it could mean he's involved... or it could mean he's a target, too."

As we continued to search the room, something caught my eye—a small, weathered journal half-buried under a pile of dusty papers. The leather cover was worn and cracked, the edges frayed from years of handling. I picked it up carefully, the pages yellowed and brittle with age.

"Look at this," I said, holding it out to the sheriff. He took it from me, his brow furrowing as he flipped through the pages, scanning the cramped handwriting and faded ink.

"This could be useful," he muttered, his eyes widening as he read further. "There are notes here about the missing people—dates, locations, and strange symbols. Whoever wrote this knew something—or was right in the middle of it."

Micky leaned in, his interest sharpening. "What does it say?"

The sheriff shook his head slightly, still reading. "It's a mix of diary entries and research. There are mentions of the abandoned factory, the old campsite, and... here." He paused, his finger tracing over a line on the page. "It mentions Roy—there's something about him being watched, and then..." The sheriff's voice trailed off, his expression darkening. "This isn't just a record of what happened. It's a plan—someone's been plotting this for a long time."

The revelation sent a shiver down my spine. The journal felt like a glimpse into a mind twisted with obsession and malice—someone who had been carefully orchestrating terror for years.

"About ten years ago, we had at least twenty women go missing, and their cases were never solved," the sheriff explained, his voice tense. "Now, it's starting again."

"Oh my gosh, I forgot all about that," Gail gasped, her hand covering her mouth.

The sheriff's eyes darted around the room, and he snapped the journal shut. "We need to get out of here," he said, his voice urgent and tight. "It's not safe."

Without another word, we all turned and hurried toward the exit, the creaking floorboards underfoot amplifying the growing dread. The cold, musty air seemed to press in around us, as if the very walls were closing in, trying to keep us trapped.

As we made our way back upstairs, a sudden movement caught my eye. A figure came rushing toward us. It was a woman, her face pale and drawn, her eyes wide with terror. My heart jumped when I recognized her—it was Firecracker, the bakery manager from Berry's Bayou Market. Her disheveled appearance and the panic in her eyes told us something was terribly wrong.

"Help me," Firecracker whispered, collapsing onto the floor, her breath ragged. "He's coming for me."

"Who's coming?" Gail asked, her voice trembling with fear.

Firecracker's eyes darted frantically around the room as she gasped, "*He is*—the one who took Cathy and the others. He's after me too."

The sheriff knelt beside her, trying to calm her down, but the sheer panic in her eyes was contagious, seeping into the rest of us. The dread that hung in the air felt almost suffocating.

"We need to go, now," the sheriff ordered, his voice sharp with urgency.

He quickly helped Firecracker to her feet, and we rushed outside into the humid, balmy night. As we piled into the sheriff's car, the uneasy silence was broken only by our ragged breathing. I couldn't shake the feeling that we weren't alone, that hidden eyes were watching us from the shadows, waiting for the right moment to strike. The hairs on the back of my neck stood on end as we sped away from the mill, but the terror clung to us, refusing to be left behind.

~ 19 ~

FIRECRACKER'S REVELATION!

I sat on the hard wooden bench outside the sheriff's office, my small legs swinging nervously above the floor. My heart pounded in my chest, each beat echoing the ominous feeling that had settled over Bayou Vista like a storm cloud. The air was thick with tension and fear, the kind that made the hairs on the back of my neck stand on end.

I watched as the sheriff gently guided Stefanie "Firecracker" into his office. Her normally bright and fierce demeanor was gone, replaced with a haunted, hollow look. Her clothes were messy, and she clutched her arms around herself like she was trying to hold it together. The door closed with a heavy thud behind them, shutting us out from whatever grim conversation was about to unfold.

Jill and Tricia quietly came and sat down beside me, their faces pale, their eyes wide with the same fear that was gnawing at me. None of us spoke at first; the silence filled with the distant hum of a ceiling fan and the muffled voices coming from inside the office.

"What do you think happened to her?" Jill finally whispered, her voice trembling.

I swallowed hard, staring at the closed door. "I don't know," I whispered back. "But whatever it is, it's bad. I've never seen Firecracker look so scared."

Tricia shivered and pulled her knees up to her chest. "Do you think it's him? Roy?" she asked, her voice barely audible.

"I don't know," I replied, trying to keep my voice steady despite the fear gripping my heart. "But whatever it was, I hope she saw Roy's face and tells the sheriff the truth."

Inside the office, the sheriff leaned back in his chair, his expression a mix of concern and curiosity. Stefanie sat across from him, her hands trembling slightly as she tried to hold herself together.

"Tell me again, Stefanie," the sheriff urged gently. "Start from the beginning."

Stefanie took a deep breath, her eyes darting around the room like she was still trapped in that moment. "I was at Jason's Bar, just having a drink, nothing out of the ordinary. When I left, I felt someone grab me from behind. Before I knew it, everything went black."

The sheriff nodded, encouraging her to continue. "And when you woke up?"

"I was in the bed of a black pickup," Stefanie's voice wavered, her hands twisting in her lap. "It was parked outside the old mill. I looked around, but I didn't see anyone. I was so scared... I ran inside the mill, and that's when I saw you."

The sheriff's eyes narrowed as he absorbed her words. "A black pickup, you say? Roy owns a black truck. You didn't see the driver's face?"

Stefanie shook her head quickly, her eyes filling with tears. "No, he had a mask on. But it wasn't Roy. The guy was too fat to be Roy. Roy's tall and skinny. I've known him for years. This guy was built different—heavy, slow. It wasn't him."

The sheriff rubbed his chin thoughtfully, the gears in his mind visibly turning. "Roy does have a black pickup," he muttered to himself. "But if it wasn't him... Jason might have more answers than he's letting on. I think I need to have another talk with him."

Through the small window in the door, I saw the sheriff, his brow furrowed with deep concern as he scribbled something in his notebook. My thoughts swirled with unanswered questions—who was this masked man? Could Roy really be behind all of this, or was someone else pulling the strings in a twisted game in Bayou Vista?

Before I could lose myself in the whirlwind of worries, Taylor and Laurrie from Berry's Market burst into the office, rushing over to check on their co-worker. They quickly exchanged hugs with her before the sheriff gestured for them to sit down. Taking seats beside Firecracker, they held her hands while the sheriff pressed on with his questions.

I was still trying to make sense of it all when I felt a tap on my shoulder. Startled, I turned to find Micky standing there. His usual jovial expression had vanished, replaced with a look of genuine concern.

"Everything okay, kiddo?" Micky asked softly.

I shook my head, "No, Micky. It's not okay. Stefanie's saying it might not be Roy, but someone else."

Micky's expression darkened. "That's what I was afraid of," he muttered under his breath, almost to himself. He glanced at the sheriff's office door, then back at me, his eyes softening. "Listen, don't worry too much."

"Girls," Gail said, her voice tinged with the same weariness we all felt. "I'm going to Brenda's coffee shop to meet Patricia and Margie and fill them in on what's happening. You all can go with Micky, and I'll pick you up when I'm done."

None of us argued; we just nodded quietly. Micky gave Gail a reassuring nod before turning to us. "Let's go, girls," he said softly, his usual playful tone replaced with something far more serious.

We followed Micky away from the sheriff's office, and as we neared his store, I noticed a woman standing by the door. Her eyes were red-rimmed, her face etched with sorrow, and she clutched a single red rose in her trembling hand. I recognized her immediately—Mary Campbell's mom. The weight of grief hung around her like a shadow, and just seeing her sent a chill through me.

"Hello, Micky," she said, her voice thick with emotion, a strained whisper as if she'd been crying for hours. "I was hoping to speak with you."

Micky's expression softened, his usual cheer replaced by deep concern. He nodded solemnly. "Of course, Mrs. Campbell. Let's go inside."

As we followed them into the store, I could feel the tension radiating off Mrs. Campbell, like she was holding back something heavy. She gripped the rose so tightly that her knuckles were white, as if it was the only thing anchoring her in place.

Mrs. Campbell looked at Micky, her eyes filled with desperation. "I need to talk to Mary. Please, I have to know if she's okay. I'm having such a terrible day, and I just need to feel that she's close."

Micky took a deep breath and nodded, his eyes soft with understanding. "Mary is always with you, Mrs. Campbell. She's holding a red rose, her favorite flower. She loves sitting in the chair by the window, looking out at the ocean."

Tears welled up in Mrs. Campbell's eyes, and her lips trembled as she tried to smile. "That's my favorite place to sit too. It's my reading nook," she said softly, her voice thick with emotion. She glanced down at the red rose in her hand and smiled faintly. "That's why I brought this. I wanted her to have it."

"She knows," Micky said gently. "And she says she loves you very much."

Mrs. Campbell's face crumpled as tears streamed down her cheeks. "Please," she whispered, her voice barely holding together. "Tell me how she died. Did she suffer?"

Micky's expression grew somber, and he shook his head slightly. "Please understand, I'd rather not go into that," he replied softly. "Just know that she's at peace now."

A heavy silence settled in the room as Mrs. Campbell absorbed his words. I watched the exchange, feeling a chill run down my spine. I wasn't sure whether to feel comforted or unsettled.

After a long, shaky breath, Mrs. Campbell nodded and wiped her eyes. "Thank you, Micky," she said softly, clutching the rose to her chest. She turned and walked away, leaving an air of sadness in the room like a fading echo.

The doorbell chimed as she left, the sound lingering in the stillness. I couldn't hold back my curiosity any longer. "How do you do that?" I asked, my voice hushed with awe.

Micky gave me a small, wistful smile. "It's a gift," he said simply. "But it can be heavy at times. Does it scare you?"

"Not at all," I said, shaking my head. "It's fascinating. But... the old mill scares me." I paused, thinking about the nagging feeling that had been growing stronger lately. "I keep thinking about the old campground. I don't know why."

Micky's smile faded as he considered my words. "The campground?" he echoed, his eyes narrowing in thought. "Sometimes our instincts pull us toward places we're meant to remember or confront."

A shiver ran down my spine at his words.

"Whatever it is," Micky continued, his voice steady but serious, "we're all in this together."

Just then, Gail arrived to pick us up. "Come on, girls, time to go," she said, ushering us toward the door. Micky gave her a reassuring nod as we left, but the worry in his eyes lingered.

Once we were in the car, the drive was quiet. Gail focused on the road while I stared out the window, replaying everything that had happened.

We dropped Tricia off first. Her house was warm and inviting, with lights glowing from the windows. "I'm sorry for being so late," Gail apologized as Tricia's parents met us at the door. "Tomorrow is a school day, and I didn't mean to keep them out so long."

Tricia's mother smiled warmly, her face full of understanding. "It's alright, Gail. We know things have been tough. You take care."

Tricia waved goodbye before running inside, her mom standing on the porch, watching us pull away.

Next, we headed to Jill's house. As we pulled up, her mom was already at the front door, waving with a welcoming smile. Jill hopped out, calling a quick "Thanks!"

before dashing up the steps. Her mom gave Gail a friendly wave before closing the door behind them.

With both girls dropped off, it was just Gail and me. The tension of the day seemed to ease as we drove in silence, the familiar route home bringing a small sense of comfort. When we finally pulled into the driveway, Gail parked the car and turned to me, her eyes clouded with worry.

"The sheriff told me Micky doesn't think it's Roy," she said quietly, as if hesitant to even say it out loud. "But he's got to be involved somehow. If he's not behind all of this, then why is he on the run?"

I stared out the window at my old house, its darkened windows staring back like cold eyes. Even though I couldn't see inside, the memory of that place still sent shivers down my spine. The thought of going back there made me grateful that I didn't have to. I reached into my pocket and pulled out the wishing stone, rubbing its smooth surface with my thumb. It had become a small ritual that gave me comfort. There was something almost magical about it, like it was protecting me.

Gail noticed the movement, her eyes softening as she watched me. She didn't say anything for a moment, just letting the silence stretch between us, peaceful and reassuring. Finally, she sighed, her shoulders relaxing a bit. "Let's get inside. It's been a long day."

I nodded, clutching the stone tightly as we stepped out of the car and made our way to the front door. The house greeted us with warm light spilling from the windows, the smell of something faintly sweet lingering in the air. Inside, the familiar walls and cozy furniture felt like a sanctuary, wrapping us in a comforting embrace. The shadows that had followed us all day seemed to fade, replaced by a sense of safety and warmth that only home could bring.

As we settled in, I couldn't help but feel a deep sense of gratitude that Gail and I were together and safe—for now.

~ 20 ~

ANOTHER DAY AT SCHOOL

The morning sun peeked over the horizon, casting long shadows across Bayou Vista. I trudged to school beside Gail, my backpack feeling heavier than usual. The early light made everything look different, almost magical, but it couldn't chase away the nervous flutter in my stomach.

"I'll pick you up after school," Gail reminded me. "And remember, don't go anywhere alone!"

Everyone around me was super excited about Halloween, but I couldn't shake the dark thoughts clouding my mind. The old mill, Roy, the campground—what happened there that terrifies me to my very core?

As I entered the schoolyard, kids were already chatting about their costumes and the haunted hayfield trip Mrs. Staggs had planned for tomorrow.

"It's not really haunted," I heard Tricia explaining to a group of wide-eyed first-graders. "Just people with masks chasing you around."

I forced a smile and waved at Tricia and Jill, but my mind was far away. Memories of Roy haunted me—the way he'd grab me, leaving me too scared to move. All the times he hit me and locked me in the closet. All the awful names he called me. His voice still echoed in my head, and I couldn't shake the way he'd look at me with those mean eyes. Is he really gone for good?

"Hey, Loretta!" Jill's voice snapped me out of my thoughts. "You okay?"

"Yeah," I lied. "Just tired."

"You sure?" Tricia asked, her eyes searching mine. "You've seemed... off."

"I'm fine," I insisted, not wanting to drag them into my worries. "Really."

The bell rang, signaling the start of another school day. As we headed inside, Mrs. Staggs greeted us with her usual enthusiasm, but even her bright smile couldn't lift my spirits.

"Good morning, class!" she called out. "I hope everyone is excited about our haunted hayfield trip tomorrow!"

The class erupted in cheers and chatter, but I remained silent, my mind still lingering on Roy and the previous night's events. The lunch bell rang, startling me, as the morning flew by in a blur.

During lunch, I sat with Jill and Tricia, picking at my food. They were discussing their Halloween costumes, but I couldn't focus.

"Loretta," Jill said suddenly, "are you coming to the hayfield tomorrow?"

I nodded absentmindedly. "Yeah, I guess."

"You don't sound too excited," Tricia observed, raising an eyebrow.

"It's just... everything that's been happening," I admitted quietly. "The old mill, Roy, the campground—it's all so creepy."

"Oh my God," Tricia said, shuddering. "The old mill gave me nightmares last night."

"I know," Jill murmured, her voice dropping to a whisper. "It's really scary. But we've got to try and have some fun, right?"

"Yeah," I sighed. "I'll try."

The afternoon passed uneventfully, and soon enough, the final bell rang. I gathered my things and headed out to meet Gail, who was waiting in the car. As soon as I got in, I could tell something was wrong.

"What's going on?" I asked, dread creeping into my voice.

Gail glanced at me, her expression grim. "There was another missing woman last night."

My heart skipped a beat. "Who?"

"Maria Campos from Cypress Cove," Gail replied. "She was taken from Jason's Bar."

I felt a chill run down my spine: another woman, another disappearance. The pieces of this horrifying puzzle were falling into place, and none of it made sense.

"There's going to be another town meeting this evening," Gail continued. "This one is bound to get ugly."

As we drove home, my mind raced with questions. Why was this happening? Was the monster I lived with responsible for these disappearances? And why did I feel like I was caught in the middle of something much bigger than I could understand?

Back at the house, Gail and I sat in the living room, the atmosphere heavy with unspoken fears. The evening news blared in the background, but neither of us paid it much attention.

"What do you think is going to happen at the meeting?" I asked finally.

Gail sighed. "I don't know. People are scared, and when people are scared, they can do some crazy things."

"Do you think Roy is involved?" I pressed.

"The sheriff said that Micky doesn't think it's Roy," Gail said quietly. "But he's probably involved somehow. Why is he running?"

I didn't have an answer, but the question lingered in the air between us. The more I thought about it, the more unsettled I became. Roy's black pickup, his disappearance, the eerie feeling at the old mill—it all pointed to him.

As the evening wore on, the tension grew. We both knew that the town meeting was going to be intense, filled with anger and fear. But for now, all we could do was wait.

The sun set, draping the town in a deepening twilight. Bayou Vista seemed to hold its breath, waiting for the inevitable confrontation that was sure to come. The answers we sought were close, but so was the danger.

Tomorrow, the haunted hayfield awaited. But tonight, the real horrors of Bayou Vista would come to light.

~ 21 ~

THE STORM

The town hall of Bayou Vista was already buzzing with heated conversations by the time Gail and I arrived. The building, usually reserved for mundane civic matters, felt like the epicenter of a storm tonight. Every seat was occupied, and people lined the walls, their faces tense with anticipation. The air was thick with fear and anger.

As we squeezed through the crowd, I spotted familiar faces: Lena White, the librarian; Mrs. Staggs, my teacher; and even Preacher John, who rarely left his house except to go to church. It seemed like the entire town had shown up, each person bringing their own grievances and suspicions.

Gail found a spot near the back by her friends Patricia and Margie, but I could barely see over the heads of the adults. I clung to her side, feeling the collective anxiety seep into my bones. Mayor Strittmatter, Sheriff Johnson, and Judge Hopper, sat at a long table at the front, trying to maintain order, but it was clear that things were already spiraling out of control.

The Mayor stood up, his face lined with worry. "Everyone, please, settle down. We need to address these concerns in an orderly manner."

But his words were lost in the uproar of shouting voices. People were demanding answers, their frustration boiling over after weeks of fear and uncertainty.

"What about Roy? What does he have to do with this?" Shannon yelled from the middle of the crowd.

"And what are the police doing about it?" Catrina chimed in.

"Not a damn thing!" an angry elderly man shouted from the front row, waving his cane in the air.

The sheriff, who was sitting beside the mayor, stood up and raised his hands for silence. "We're doing everything we can. But we need more information. We're working on leads—"

"Leads? That's not good enough!" shouted Mr. Berry, his face red with anger. "My daughter could be next!"

The room erupted again, people shouting over each other. I could see Jason standing off to the side, looking grim. His bar had become a focal point of suspicion, and the tension around him was palpable.

"This all started happening around Jason's Bar," LaDonna accused, pointing a shaky finger. "What's going on there?"

Jason stepped forward, his jaw clenched. "I run a respectable establishment. What happened to those women has nothing to do with my bar."

"Respectable? People get drunk and rowdy there every night!" Tanya shouted, her kind face twisted with anger.

"Jason's right!" Stefanie, also known as Firecracker, called out as she stepped up beside him. Her nickname felt ironic now, given the calm yet firm tone of her voice. "The night I was taken, it could have happened anywhere. Jason's Bar isn't to blame."

The room quieted for a moment as Stefanie spoke, her words carrying weight. She had survived an ordeal that left everyone else on edge, and her defense of Jason seemed to sway some of the crowd. But not everyone.

"We need to shut that place down until this is sorted out!" Cindy insisted, her voice quivering with a mix of fear and determination.

"That's not fair!" Matilda argued from the back. "Blaming the bar won't bring anyone back. We need to find out who's really behind this."

A woman in the front row stood up, tears streaming down her face. "My sister is missing. We can't just sit around and argue—we need to do something!"

"He murdered my daughter! Someone needs to find Roy and kill him!" shouted Mary Campbell's mom, her voice trembling with rage. "That's the only way this is going to end!"

"Kill him! Kill him!" the angry mob chanted, their voices growing louder and more menacing.

I glanced over the crowd and spotted Taylor and Laurrie standing close to Firecracker, their faces pale with fear.

The mayor slammed his fist on the table. "People, please! We can't let this spiral into vigilantism!" His voice boomed through the room as he continued, "Everyone, calm down! We need to approach this rationally and work together!"

The sheriff stepped forward, his tone firm as he tried to regain control. "I get that you're all frustrated, but shutting down businesses and taking the law into your own hands won't fix anything. We need your cooperation. If you see anything suspicious, report it immediately. That's how we'll get through this—together."

The crowd began to murmur, some nodding in agreement while others continued to grumble. The tension was palpable, and it felt like the fragile peace could shatter at any moment.

Suddenly, a loud bang echoed through the hall as Preacher John slammed his fist on a nearby table. "This isn't good enough! We're living in fear, and all we get are empty promises!"

People began to shout again, their voices merging into a chaotic roar. I clung to Gail, my heart pounding. The room was becoming a pressure cooker, and I could sense that something was about to give.

Jason stepped forward, raising his hands to address the crowd. "Listen, I understand your fear. My bar is open to everyone, and I want to help find whoever is responsible for these disappearances. Blaming each other won't get us anywhere."

Dondi scoffed. "And what are you going to do, Jason? Serve them a drink and ask them nicely to stop?"

Before Jason could respond, Kathy Berry shouted, "I saw a black pickup near the old mill last night! Isn't that Roy's truck?"

A wave of murmurs spread through the room. The sheriff's eyes narrowed, and he scanned the crowd. "Who said that? Come forward."

Kathy hesitated, then stepped into the open space. "It was me, Sheriff. I saw it. And I'm not the only one."

Brenda raised her hand, her voice steady but tense. "I saw it too. Roy's truck was parked near the bar earlier that evening."

The sheriff's expression darkened. "We've been searching for Roy, but it's like he's vanished. Jason, did you see him at your bar last night?"

Jason shook his head firmly. "No, Sheriff. If he'd been there, I would've called you right away."

"Yeah, sure you would've," someone jeered from the crowd.

"Enough!" the sheriff snapped, his patience wearing thin. "If anyone knows anything about Roy's whereabouts, now's the time to speak up."

Rosie chuckled dryly. "Well, he can't be that hard to find if his truck keeps popping up all over town, can he?"

The room fell silent, the weight of the situation sinking in. It was as if everyone collectively held their breath, waiting for the next piece of the puzzle to fall into place.

Gail squeezed my hand, her face pale. "Stay close," she whispered.

Just then, Micky broke the silence. "We can't just wait around for something to happen. We need to organize patrols, search the area, do something!"

Mrs. Staggs, near the front, stood up. "I agree. Let's form a group and start searching the town and surrounding areas. We can't leave it all to the police."

The mayor nodded, seeing the opportunity to channel the crowd's energy into something productive. "That's a good idea. We'll need volunteers to form search parties. Anyone willing to help, please step forward."

Dozens of hands shot up, people eager to take action. The room buzzed with a renewed sense of purpose, but the underlying tension remained.

As the volunteers gathered, I noticed Jason and Stefanie talking quietly. Stefanie's face was set with determination, and Jason looked equally resolved. They were planning something, and I had a feeling it involved more than just searching for Roy.

The sheriff took the microphone again. "Thank you all for your willingness to help. We'll coordinate the search efforts and keep you informed. Remember, safety in numbers. No one goes out alone."

People began to organize into groups, and the chaotic energy started to transform into a more focused determination.

Gail leaned down to whisper in my ear. "Stay close to me, Loretta."

I nodded, my grip tightening on the wishing stone in my pocket.

As the meeting continued, the discussions became more structured. The mayor assigned leaders to each group, and they began planning their search routes. But despite the semblance of order, the underlying fear and suspicion never fully dissipated.

"I want answers!" Brenda shouted, her frustration boiling over. "What's the plan if we find Roy? What if he's not alone?"

"Shoot him!" someone yelled from the crowd.

"Who said that?" the sheriff bellowed angrily, scanning the crowd.

"Listen, everyone," the mayor interjected. "We can't take the law into our own hands."

The sheriff held up his hand. "If you find Roy or anyone suspicious, don't approach them. Contact us immediately. We don't want anyone else getting hurt."

Lena stepped forward, her voice shaking. "And what about the rest of us? What can we do to stay safe?"

"Stay in groups," the sheriff advised. "Keep your homes locked, and report anything unusual. We'll have increased patrols, but we need your cooperation."

"What about Halloween night?" LaDonna demanded.

"Yes," Shannon added, her voice rising. "What about our children?"

The sheriff sighed, his shoulders heavy with the weight of the decision. "I wanted to cancel Halloween this year, but the vote was to go ahead with it. We don't believe the person behind this is targeting children, but that doesn't mean we can let our guard down. I need everyone to be extra vigilant—stick to pairs, watch out for each other, and report anything suspicious immediately."

The crowd seemed to calm slightly, but the atmosphere remained charged. The fear that had gripped Bayou Vista was far from gone, and it was clear that tonight's meeting was just the beginning of a long and difficult battle.

As the discussions continued, I overheard snippets of conversations around me. People were scared, and the uncertainty was driving them to the edge. Accusations flew, and tempers flared, but amidst the chaos, there was also a sense of community.

"We have to stick together," Dondi said, his earlier anger giving way to determination. "We can't let this tear us apart."

Jason nodded, his expression grim. "We'll get through this. But we have to be smart."

Firecracker stepped forward again, her voice firm. "Jason's right. Blaming each other won't solve anything. We need to focus on finding the truth."

The room fell silent once more, everyone absorbing her words. Stefanie's bravery and resilience seemed to galvanize the crowd, and for a moment, it felt like there was a glimmer of hope.

The mayor stood up again, addressing the room. "We'll reconvene tomorrow to assess our progress. In the meantime, stay vigilant and look out for each other."

As the meeting adjourned, the crowd began to disperse, people talking in hushed tones as they left the hall. Gail and I stayed behind, watching as the volunteers organized their groups and prepared for the search.

"Be careful," the sheriff said, shaking hands with each group leader. "We'll find whoever is responsible for this."

I looked up at Gail, my heart heavy with worry. "Do you think we'll find Roy?"

She sighed, her expression thoughtful. "I don't know, Loretta. But we have to try."

As we went home, the streets of Bayou Vista felt eerily quiet. The events of the night played over and over in my mind, each detail adding to the sense of dread that had settled in my chest.

When we finally reached our house, Gail turned to me, her face serious. "We need to be extra careful from now on. No going out alone, and always stay alert."

I nodded, understanding the gravity of her words. The town was on edge, and it felt like we were all teetering on the brink of something terrible.

Inside, the house was warm and inviting, a stark contrast to the cold fear that gripped me. I sat down on the couch, clutching the wishing stone in my hand. The familiar warmth of the stone brought a small measure of comfort, but it couldn't chase away the fear.

Gail sat beside me, her hand on my shoulder. "We'll get through this, Loretta."

I nodded, though my mind was still racing with questions. What was happening in Bayou Vista? Why were people disappearing? And what did Roy have to do with it all?

~ 22 ~

SHADOWS IN THE HAUNTED HAYFIELD

Bayou Vista was buzzing like a beehive, everyone talking about the town meeting at school. Even Mrs. Staggs, who was usually calm and collected, seemed a bit on edge. Still, she was determined that our annual haunted hayfield trip would go on. She said keeping things normal for us kids was important, even though nothing ever felt normal for me.

I was both excited and scared as I got on the bus, my backpack bouncing against my back. Matilda, our bus driver, handed each of us a small carton of orange juice. "Drink up, kiddos," she said with her usual warm smile. "It's going to be a fun trip!"

Despite everything happening in town, I loved field trips. They were a chance to escape from the usual routine. I took my seat on the bus, and Jill, Tricia, and I huddled together, whispering excitedly about the haunted hayfield and wondering what surprises might be waiting for us there.

The bus ride seemed to take forever. Outside, the fields were covered in a thick mist, and the sky was a dull gray. The hayfield was usually open only at night, but each year they made an exception and let us in during the morning. We would have lunch at the small park next door and then return to school.

When we finally arrived, Mrs. Staggs stood at the front of the bus. "Alright, everyone. Listen up! I want you to stay in groups of three at all times. Do not leave your group, no matter what. Understand?"

We all nodded and mumbled, "Yes, Mrs. Staggs." As we stepped off the bus, the hayfield loomed ahead of us, a maze of tall, twisted stacks of hay. The air smelled like damp straw and something else I couldn't quite place, something metallic and sour.

As we walked into the hayfield, I noticed a fat clown peeking at us from behind a haystack. His face was painted white, with bright red lips twisted into a grin that made my skin crawl. I nudged Jill. "Look at that clown," I whispered.

Jill squinted in the direction I was pointing. "Creepy," she muttered. "He's just part of the show."

Tricia shrugged. "They always have weird stuff at these things."

Mrs. Staggs herded us forward, reminding everyone to stick together. The hayfield was like a giant labyrinth, with narrow paths and hidden corners. We could hear the distant laughter of kids from a nearby school, mixed with the occasional shriek when someone got spooked. The Hayfield was a popular attraction, drawing schools from both Cypress Cove and Pelican Bay every year.

We were halfway through the maze when I saw the clown again, this time closer. He was watching us, his eyes glinting with something that made my stomach churn. "He's following us," I said, my voice shaking.

"Just ignore him," Jill said, though she sounded more scared than confident. "It's just part of the act."

I tried to focus on the hayfield, but the feeling of being watched was overwhelming. Every time I glanced over my shoulder, the clown was there, always just a little closer.

We turned a corner, and standing in the middle of the path was a figure in a hockey mask holding a machete. He raised the machete slowly, the blade catching the dim light, and stepped toward us.

I screamed, grabbing Jill's arm. "Run!"

We bolted down the narrow path, our hearts pounding in our chests. Behind us, we could hear the heavy footsteps of the masked figure getting closer. We turned another corner, and there was another figure—this one in a white mask. He stood still, just staring at us, his presence more terrifying than the first one.

Then it happened. We were navigating a particularly narrow path when the clown lunged out from behind a bale of hay. His fat, painted face was right in front of us, the red lips pulled back in a sinister grin. I screamed, stumbling backward.

Before any of us could react, he grabbed me, his gloved hands wrapping around my arm. I struggled, kicking and screaming, but he was strong. "Let go of me!" I yelled, my voice high with fear.

"Hey!" Jill shouted, rushing forward. Tricia was right behind her, their faces pale. The clown's grip slipped for a moment, and I wrenched myself free, falling to the ground.

Tricia was crying now, her breath coming in ragged gasps. "We need to find Mrs. Staggs!"

We stumbled through the hay maze, the figures of the clown and the masked men disappearing and reappearing in the corners of our vision. Every turn seemed to bring a new horror. We rounded a bend, and suddenly, a man with a chainsaw burst out from behind a bale of hay. The roar of the chainsaw was deafening, and he swung it wildly, the blade just inches from us.

"Go, go, go!" Jill shouted, pushing us forward. We sprinted down the path, the sound of the chainsaw chasing us, mixing with our screams.

We finally burst into a clearing, where Mrs. Staggs and some other kids were standing. "What's wrong?" she asked, her face pale.

"There's—there's people in there," I panted. "A guy with a hockey mask, another with a white mask, a clown, and a guy with a chainsaw!"

Mrs. Staggs looked around, her eyes wide with disbelief. "That can't be right. This is supposed to be a controlled environment. They knew today was for children only!"

Just then, I saw the clown again. He was standing at the edge of the clearing, his painted face grinning at us. He started walking toward us, and I felt a cold dread settle in my stomach. "It's him," I whispered. "He's the one who grabbed me."

Mrs. Staggs turned to look, her face hardening. "Everyone, stay here," she said, her voice trembling with anger. She marched over to the clown, but before she could reach him, he slipped into the shadows of the maze.

The manager of the haunted hayfield arrived, looking frazzled. "What's going on here?" he demanded.

"There are people in there scaring the kids—people who aren't supposed to be here," Mrs. Staggs said, her voice shaking with fury. "Some guy with a hockey mask, another with a white mask, a clown, and a guy with a chainsaw!"

The manager furrowed his brow, clearly puzzled. "They were scheduled to start work tonight. And we definitely don't have a clown on staff."

"But we saw them!" Tricia protested, her voice rising with urgency. "They were real, I swear!"

"I saw the clown myself," Mrs. Staggs interjected, her tone sharp with frustration. "It wasn't just a figment of our imagination. Something's not right here."

"The clown grabbed Loretta!" Jill said, pointing at me. "He just grabbed her and wouldn't let go!"

"I don't know who you saw, but we don't have any clowns," he said, his voice shaky. "There's no clown on our payroll. As for the rest of the crew, they were told today was for children, so they shouldn't be here. Only the family-friendly characters are around today."

I was still shaking, tears streaming down my face. "He was real," I insisted. "He grabbed me."

Just then, the man with the chainsaw emerged from the maze.

"Hey, Billy!" the manager called out, waving him over.

Tricia and Jill quickly ducked behind Mrs. Staggs.

"Why are you here?" the manager demanded, his voice laced with irritation.

Billy shrugged, looking confused. "I got a call last night. They said you wanted us here first thing this morning."

The manager ran a hand through his hair, glancing around anxiously as if expecting the clown to materialize at any moment. "I'm sorry," he said, his voice tense. "It was supposed to be just like every other year – ghosts, skeletons, and witches."

"Well, we better leave," Mrs. Staggs said, her voice firm. "These children have been traumatized enough."

"I'm truly sorry, everyone," the manager apologized, his face etched with regret.

We huddled together, our hearts pounding. The hayfield, once a place of harmless scares, now felt like a nightmare.

The bus ride back to school was silent. Matilda kept glancing at us in the rearview mirror, her usual smile replaced by a worried frown.

Back at school, the students couldn't stop talking about what had happened. My friends gathered around me, offering words of comfort.

"That was so scary," Tricia said, her voice trembling. "I'm glad you got away."

Jill nodded, her expression serious. "We need to stick together. Whatever's going on, we can't let it scare us apart."

I managed a weak smile. "Thanks, guys. I don't know what I would have done without you."

Mrs. Staggs was deep in conversation with the principal and the town sheriff. "We need to find out who's behind this and identify that clown," she said, her voice steady and resolute. "We can't allow anyone to terrorize our children like this."

The sheriff nodded, looking grim. "We'll investigate. In the meantime, everyone needs to be extra cautious."

Parents huddled together, exchanging worried glances. "This town used to be so safe," one mother said, shaking her head. "I don't know what's happening anymore."

The principal stood by the pickup area, trying to reassure everyone. "We'll be increasing security to ensure the safety of our children. But we need everyone's cooperation. If you notice anything unusual, please report it immediately."

Gail rushed over to me, her face filled with concern. "Are you okay, honey? Mrs. Staggs told me what happened."

I nodded, still trembling. "It was so scary, Gail. There were all these men – one with a machete, one wearing a creepy mask, and another with a chainsaw. But the worst was the clown... he grabbed me."

Gail's eyes widened. "A clown? What do you mean he grabbed you?"

I took a deep breath, trying to steady myself. "He was following us through the maze. At first, we thought he was part of the act, but then he got closer and closer. He grabbed my arm and wouldn't let go."

Gail hugged me tightly. "I'm so sorry you had to go through that. Did Mrs. Staggs do anything?"

"Yeah, she tried to confront the clown, but he disappeared into the maze before she could reach him."

Gail looked around, her expression turning from concern to determination. "We're going to get to the bottom of this. No one should be scaring kids like that."

I shook my head, wiping away the tears from my eyes.

Gail sighed. "Alright, let's get you home. And don't worry, I won't let anything like this happen again."

I nodded, feeling a bit more at ease. "Thanks, Gail. I'm just glad it's over."

Gail gave me another reassuring hug. "Me too, honey. Me too."

When we got home, I noticed something strange. A small package was sitting on the front porch, wrapped in plain brown paper. My heart skipped a beat. "Wait here," Gail told me, approaching cautiously.

She picked up the package, her hands trembling. There was no return address, just like the last time. She opened the box, identical to the previous one. Her eyes scanned the paper inside, and she quickly glanced around.

I gasped. "What is it?"

"Nothing for you to worry about," Gail replied, her voice barely above a whisper. She quickly crumpled the paper and stuffed it into her pocket. "You've been through enough already," Gail said, her tone gentle yet firm.

That night, I lay in bed, unable to sleep. Everything that happened today kept playing over and over in my head. The clown's creepy face haunted my thoughts, making me shiver. The scare at the hayfield had made everything so much scarier in Bayou Vista. It wasn't just whispers and rumors anymore; it felt real, and everyone knew it.

~ 23 ~

CLUES AND THE CLOWN

The morning air was thick with the promise of another sweltering day in Bayou Vista. The weather this time of year, much like the monster haunting our town, was unpredictable and oppressive. Gail drove me to school, her fingers tapping nervously on the steering wheel. The radio was tuned to the local news, and the reporter's voice was tense as he recounted the latest disappearance.

"Bayou Vista has another missing woman. Denise Benoit was last seen at Jason's Bar late last night. Authorities are urging anyone with information to come forward…"

Gail gasped, her knuckles white as she gripped the steering wheel. "Oh my God," she whispered. "How many more?"

I tuned out the rest, my thoughts drifting back to the creepy clown I'd seen in the haunted hayfield and the chilling note we'd found in the package: '*TICK TOCK.*' I couldn't shake the feeling that these events were connected somehow.

"Are you okay, Loretta?" Gail asked, glancing at me with concern.

"Yeah, I'm fine," I lied, forcing a smile. But I wasn't fine. Not at all.

When we pulled up to the school, I grabbed my backpack and gave Gail a quick hug. "Thanks for the ride. See you later."

"Alright, sweetie," Gail said with a warm smile, waving at Mrs. Staggs. "Be extra careful out there today, okay?"

I nodded, feeling the weight of her words.

As I walked into the schoolyard, my mind was a whirlwind of thoughts. Gail's friend, Patricia, told her that Sheriff Johnson had searched Roy's house again, and I knew they were looking for him, but something still felt off. And now, another woman was missing, last seen at Jason's Bar, and just like that, she was gone.

In class, I could barely concentrate. Mrs. Staggs' voice was a distant hum, and the words on the blackboard blurred together. All I could think about was the ever-growing list of missing people. It started with just four, but now it's Roy, Mary, Cathy, Patti, Maria—and now Denise. What was happening to our town?

At recess, I found Tricia and Jill by the swings. They were speaking in hushed voices, their faces pale with fear.

"Did you hear about Denise?" I asked, joining them.

Tricia nodded, her eyes wide. "My mom said the sheriff's been searching everywhere, but there's no trace of her."

"I'm really scared," Jill admitted, her voice trembling.

"I know," I agreed, the knot of fear in my stomach tightening.

"Do you think Roy is the one dressed like the clown?" Tricia asked.

"Who else would be chasing after Loretta like that?" Jill replied, her voice barely above a whisper. "He's a—"

She cut herself off, unable to finish the thought, but we all knew what she meant. Roy was a monster, the lowest of the low. The fear he'd brought into my life clung to me like a dark shadow, creeping into every corner of my mind. None of us felt safe anymore.

The bell rang, signaling the end of recess, and we trudged back inside. The rest of the day passed in a blur, and before I knew it, Gail was picking me up from school.

"Did you have a good day?" she asked as I climbed into the car.

"Yeah, it was okay," I replied, trying to sound normal.

As we drove home, I noticed Sheriff Johnson's car parked in front of my old house. My heart skipped a beat. *What were they doing now?*

"Gail, can we go over there for a minute?" I asked, my curiosity taking over.

She looked at me with concern but nodded. "I guess it'll be alright... just for a minute."

We got out of the car and slowly approached the house. I spotted Sheriff Johnson and his deputy deep in conversation on the porch. At first, they didn't notice us, but then the sheriff's eyes met mine.

"Loretta, what are you doing here?" he asked, surprised.

"I was just curious," I admitted. "Did you find anything?"

The sheriff sighed, shaking his head. "No, nothing yet. But we're not giving up. We'll find out what's going on, I promise."

I nodded, a mix of relief and frustration swirling within me. As I turned to leave, something shiny caught my eye beneath the porch. My heart raced as I bent down for a closer look. It was a ladies' wristwatch. I picked it up, feeling its cold weight in my hand, a chill running down my spine. Whose watch was this? And why was it here?

"*TICK TOCK*," I whispered to myself, the words sending a shiver down my spine.

"Loretta, come on, we need to go," Gail said. "What is that?"

"I found this under the porch," I said, showing her the watch. "It has the initials P. W. engraved on the back."

"That's creepy," Gail said, her eyes wide. "Give it to the sheriff."

I stared at the wristwatch in my hand, its face glinting in the sunlight. It was unmistakably a woman's watch, delicate and adorned with tiny rhinestones. My breath caught in my throat. Could this belong to Patti Williams?

"It's Patti's watch," I whispered, my voice shaky with both fear and excitement.

Sheriff Johnson turned sharply at the sound of my voice, his eyes narrowing as he approached. "Loretta, what do you have there?" he asked, his tone urgent.

I held out the watch, my hand shaking slightly. "I found it under the porch," I said, my voice barely above a whisper.

Sheriff Johnson's face tightened as he took the watch from me, examining it closely. "This... this could be a major clue," he said, looking back at the deputy. "We need to search the house again."

All around us, neighbors were gathering, whispering like a swarm of angry bees. Preacher John was on his porch with the mayor, both looking really worried. Everyone was watching, and rumors were flying as the sheriff and his deputy went back inside to search again.

I scanned the crowd, my eyes jumping from one face to another. The tension was so thick it felt like a heavy blanket pressing down on all of us. The search felt like it was taking forever. My heart pounded in my chest as I tried to make sense of everything. Then, out of the corner of my eye, I saw him—the clown. He stood by some tall bushes next to Preacher John's house, his painted face grinning eerily in the evening light.

"Gail, look!" I gasped, tugging at her sleeve and pointing towards the bushes.

But when Gail turned to look, the clown was gone. She frowned, her eyes sweeping over the empty space.

"Loretta, there's nothing there," she said, her voice gentle but firm.

"He was there, I swear!" I insisted, my heart racing even faster. "The clown from the hayfield! He was right there!"

Gail glanced at me with concern, her brow furrowing. "Let's not jump to conclusions, okay? It's been a stressful day."

Preacher John approached us, noticing the tension. "This search sure is taking longer than expected. They must be onto something." He looked at me with curiosity. "What's wrong?"

"Loretta saw the clown standing by your house just now—the same one from the hayfield," Gail explained, pointing toward the bushes.

The preacher's expression tightened as he quickly signaled the mayor. Together, they rushed to the spot Gail pointed out. They combed the area, searching all around the house, but came up empty-handed. Preacher John shook his head as he signaled back to Gail, indicating that nothing was there.

"Honey, if he was there, he's gone now," Gail said softly.

I wanted to argue, to make them believe me, but the words stuck in my throat. I just stood there, a cold chill creeping up my spine. I knew what I saw—the clown was real, and somehow, he was connected to all of this—the missing people, the watch, the sinister note. But how?

Finally, the door of Roy's house creaked open, and Sheriff Johnson and his deputy emerged, their faces grim. "No sign of Roy," the sheriff announced, shaking his head. "But this watch... it's a lead. We'll follow it."

The crowd murmured, and I felt a mixture of relief and frustration wash over me. We had a clue, but we were no closer to finding Roy or any of the missing women.

As the neighbors began to disperse, I couldn't shake the feeling that we were being watched. I glanced around nervously, my eyes lingering on the bushes where the clown had stood. Had I imagined it? Or was he still out there, lurking in the shadows?

"Come on, Loretta," Gail said, gently steering me towards her house. "Let's go home."

I nodded, my mind racing with all the strange things that had happened.

When we got to Gail's house, she made us both some hot cocoa. We sat at the kitchen table, the warm, sweet smell filling the air. I stirred my cocoa absentmindedly, staring at the swirling chocolate.

"Are you alright, Loretta?" Gail asked, her voice soft and concerned.

"I don't know," I admitted, taking a sip of the cocoa. "Everything feels so weird. The missing women, the watch, the clown... it's like a scary movie."

Gail reached across the table and squeezed my hand. "We'll figure this out," she said. "The sheriff is doing everything he can, and we'll stay safe. You're not alone in this."

After cocoa, we tried to watch a movie to distract ourselves. Gail put on one of my favorite comedies, but I couldn't focus. My mind kept drifting back to the watch and the clown. Every noise outside made me jump, and the movie's bright colors and cheerful characters felt out of place with the darkness in my head.

When the movie ended, Gail suggested we make a quick and simple dinner. We fixed sandwiches and had some fruit, eating in a comfortable silence. Gail talked a bit about her day and some funny stories from her childhood, trying to lighten the mood. I smiled and laughed, but the worry still gnawed at the back of my mind.

After dinner, we played a game of cards. Gail taught me a new game called Rummy, and we laughed as I tried to remember all the rules. It was nice to focus on something normal for a while, but as the game went on, I found myself glancing out the window, half-expecting to see the clown's painted face staring back at me.

Finally, it was time for bed. Gail tucked me in, and we said our goodnights. She left the door slightly open, just the way I liked it, with the hallway light casting a warm glow into the room.

But as I lay in bed, I couldn't relax. I clutched Mr. Teddy and my wishing stone tightly. The moonlight streamed through the window, casting eerie shadows on the walls. The room felt too quiet, too still.

"*TICK TOCK*," I whispered to myself, feeling the weight of the mystery pressing down on me. I wondered if Roy was out there somewhere. And what about the clown? Why did he keep appearing? What did he want?

My eyelids grew heavy, and I finally drifted off to sleep. My dreams were like stepping into a nightmare. Clowns with creepy grins danced around me, their painted faces twisted and terrifying. The sound of a ticking clock echoed in the darkness, getting louder and louder. I felt like something or someone was lurking just out of sight, always watching me, waiting to pounce. The shadows seemed to move and whisper, sending chills down my spine. It was like being trapped in a scary movie I couldn't escape from.

~ 24 ~

THE CLASS PARTY

The first light of dawn filtered through my window as the distant cries of gulls stirred me awake. It was Friday, the day of our class Halloween party. With tomorrow being Halloween, Mrs. Staggs hoped that letting us wear our costumes today would lift everyone's spirits. My ghost outfit was ready and waiting, carefully draped across my chair.

"Are you sure you want to go, Loretta?" Gail asked as she handed me a plate of scrambled eggs for breakfast. She sounded really worried.

"Yeah, I think it'll be fun," I replied, trying to sound more cheerful than I felt. "Maybe it'll take my mind off things."

Gail smiled, but her eyes still held that worried look. "Alright then, just remember to have fun and try to relax."

As we drove to school, I couldn't shake the uneasy feeling in my stomach. Halloween was usually one of my favorite times of the year, but this year felt different. With Roy on the loose, the recent disappearances, and that creepy note, everything had taken on an unsettling, eerie vibe.

When we arrived at school, I saw Tricia and Jill waiting for me on the steps, both dressed in their costumes. Jill dressed up as a witch, complete with a pointy hat and a broomstick, while Tricia went as a pirate, sporting an eye patch and a plastic parrot perched on her shoulder.

"Hey, Loretta!" Jill called out, waving her broomstick. "Ready for the party?"

"Yeah," I said, forcing a smile. "Let's make the most of it."

"Arr..." Tricia chimed in, completing her pirate persona with a playful snarl.

As we walked into the school, I couldn't shake the feeling of unease. Every clown costume I saw sent shivers down my spine, reminding me of the creepy clown that seemed to haunt my thoughts. But I tried to push those fears aside and focus on having fun.

The party was in full swing by the time we got to our classroom. Mrs. Staggs had decorated the room with orange and black streamers, paper bats, and a big plastic cauldron filled with candy. There were games and music, and everyone seemed to be in high spirits.

"Alright, class," Mrs. Staggs announced, clapping her hands to get our attention. "It's time for the costume parade! Everyone line up and show off your costumes!"

We lined up and paraded around the classroom, showing off our costumes to each other. It was fun, and for a little while, I managed to forget about the strange events that had been plaguing our town.

After the parade, we played games like bobbing for apples and pin the tail on the donkey. The room was filled with laughter, and I even managed to win a few pieces of candy. But every now and then, I would catch sight of a clown costume and feel that familiar chill run down my spine.

When the party finally ended, I had a bag full of candy and a smile on my face. Gail picked me up from school, and I could tell she was relieved to see me in good spirits.

"Did you have fun?" she asked as we drove to Tanya's Crawfish Shack for dinner.

"Yeah, it was great," I said, holding up my bag of candy. "Look how much candy I got!"

Gail laughed. "That's a lot of candy! We might have to ration it out over the next few weeks."

When we arrived at Tanya's Crawfish Shack, we were greeted by the delicious smell of seafood. Gail's friends Patricia and Margie were already there, sitting at a table and chatting animatedly.

"Hi, Loretta!" Patricia said, waving us over. "You look adorable in your ghost costume!"

"Thanks," I said, feeling a little embarrassed but happy for the compliment.

"Loretta," Gail chuckled, "take off your costume so you can actually eat."

Her friends laughed, and I sheepishly pulled off the sheet, joining in on the laughter. We ordered our food and settled in for what was supposed to be a cozy meal. The adults chatted away about everything from town gossip to upcoming events, and I listened, soaking in the warmth and normalcy of the moment. But beneath it all, a faint sense of unease lingered, like a shadow in the back of my mind that I couldn't quite shake.

After dinner, Gail suggested we stop by Micky's shop. "He might have some new items for Halloween," she said with a smile. "And I think you'll enjoy it."

I agreed, curious about what we might find there. When we arrived, the shop was bustling with people, most of them the parents of the missing women. It seemed like the whole town had gathered there.

Micky was behind the counter, talking to Mary Campbell's mom. He looked up as we walked in and gave us a warm smile. "Good evening, Ladies! What can I do for you today?"

"We're just browsing," Margie replied.

Gail and her friends wandered off, leaving me to explore on my own. I wandered around, looking at the strange items and wondering what secrets they might hold. I couldn't help but eavesdrop on the conversation between two customers.

"...he has an extraordinary gift," one woman was saying. "He can talk to the dead."

My curiosity piqued, I moved closer, pretending to examine a shelf of knick-knacks.

"He helped me contact my sister," the woman continued. "It was... comforting, to say the least."

Just like my mom. The thought flashed through my mind.

Before I could dwell on it further, I saw Micky with a worried look on his face. "Loretta, can I talk to you?"

I nodded, my voice trembling slightly. "Of course, Micky."

"What's troubling you?" Micky asked gently. "I can tell something is wrong."

I glanced around nervously, lowering my voice to a whisper. "The clown at the Haunted Hayfield... he grabbed me. And now, I think he's following me."

Micky's face grew grim.

I pulled the small, smooth stone from my pocket. "I'm carrying the wishing stone," I said. "Ever since you gave it to me, it revealed Roy's secret and kept him away from me. Maybe it will protect me from the clown too."

Micky sighed and gently put a hand on my shoulder. "Listen, Loretta, the stone is powerful, but you've got to be careful. Keep it close, but don't let fear take over. Fear can mess with your head and make you see things that aren't there."

I nodded, trying to take in his advice. "I think that's what Gail was trying to tell me the other day too."

"Just be careful, though," he said with a small, worried smile.

"Okay," I agreed. "Does Mary Campbell's mom come here every day?"

He sighed and nodded. "Yeah, she does. Poor woman—still holding out hope."

As we left the shop, a sudden, chilling scream pierced the night air. "Help! Somebody help me!"

"Hurry, get in the car!" Gail shouted. We dashed toward the source of the scream, which seemed to be coming from near Jason's Bar.

The bar's parking lot was eerily quiet as we approached. An open car door creaked in the wind, and a woman's purse lay discarded on the ground. The woman who had screamed was nowhere to be seen.

Gail's face was set in a determined frown as she instructed, "Loretta, stay close." She pushed open the door to Jason's Bar and rushed inside, calling out, "Jason! We need help!"

Jason, the bar's owner, hurried over. "What's going on?"

"We heard a woman outside screaming for help, but now she's gone," Gail explained quickly. "Her purse is out there, but she's nowhere to be found."

Jason didn't hesitate. He grabbed his phone and dialed the sheriff while leading us back outside. Sheriff Johnson arrived within minutes, his expression a mix of frustration and determination.

He knelt by the purse, rifling through it until he found an ID. "Julie Broussard," he muttered, shaking his head. "Damn it, not another one."

Determined to find her, Sheriff Johnson and his deputies spread out, searching the area with flashlights and calling out Julie's name. The moonlight bathed the scene in an eerie glow.

We waited until the sheriff and deputies finally gave up the search. The night air was damp, and the streets were eerily quiet as we walked back to Gail's car. I couldn't shake the creepy feeling that someone was watching me.

On the drive home, Gail was unusually quiet, her thoughts clearly on the evening's events. I couldn't blame her. The things we had witnessed were beyond anything we had ever imagined.

"Are you okay, honey?" Gail asked gently.

"I can't believe there's another missing woman," I said, my voice trembling.

"I know," Gail replied, trying to reassure me. "Hopefully, the sheriff will figure it out soon."

When we got home, Gail tucked me into bed, but there was a hint of urgency in her usual comforting touch. "Try to get some rest, Loretta," she said softly, brushing a strand of hair from my face. "Tomorrow is Halloween, and we'll make sure it's a good day, okay?"

I nodded, feeling super tired but too wound up to sleep. "Goodnight, Gail," I said, trying to hide my fear.

"Goodnight, sweetie," she replied, turning off the light and closing the door halfway.

~ 25 ~

HALLOWEEN MORNING

The next morning, I woke up to the sound of the TV blaring in the living room. As I shuffled into the room, still rubbing sleep from my eyes, I saw Gail staring at the screen, her face pale. The news anchor was talking about the missing woman, Julie Broussard, who had disappeared from Jason's Bar last night.

"Julie Broussard was taken from Jason's Bar last night," the anchor said, showing a picture of Julie smiling. "Authorities are urging anyone with information to come forward."

I felt a shiver run down my spine. Gail noticed me and quickly turned off the TV.

"Morning, honey," she said, trying to sound cheerful. "Patricia and Margie are coming over to help make popcorn balls for the trick-or-treaters tonight."

I nodded, still feeling the unease from the previous night. It wasn't long before Patricia and Margie arrived, bringing bags of ingredients and their own nervous energy.

The kitchen soon filled with the smell of melting butter and caramel as the three women started making popcorn balls. I sat at the table, pretending to read a book, but really, I was listening to their conversation.

"Did you hear about Julie?" Patricia said, her voice low and serious.

"Of course," Gail replied with a sigh. "We were there last night."

"What?" Patricia shrieked in shock.

"Yes," Gail replied, "it's just awful. Another woman is gone. What is happening to our town?"

Margie nodded, looking worried. "And at Jason's Bar, no less. You'd think people would stop going there, especially with everyone being taken from that place."

Gail shook her head. "I just don't understand it. First, it was Roy, now this. It's like we're cursed."

They continued to gossip, their voices a mix of fear and curiosity. They talked about the other missing women, Jason's Bar, and then, inevitably, Roy.

"I never did trust Roy," Margie said, her tone hushed. "Always seemed a bit off to me."

"Yeah, remember that time at the town fair?" Patricia added, shaking her head. "He was lurking around the cotton candy stand, just watching everyone. Gave me the creeps."

Gail nodded thoughtfully. "And he always seemed to know things, like secrets. I don't know how he did it, but it was unsettling."

They were all silent for a moment; the only sound was the crackling of the popcorn on the stove. I could feel the tension in the air, thick and heavy, as if it was something you could touch.

Margie broke the silence, her voice barely above a whisper. "Do you think Roy had something to do with the disappearances?"

Gail hesitated, then shook her head. "I don't want to believe that. But we can't ignore the possibility."

"Poor Loretta," Patricia whispered. "I can't even begin to imagine what she went through. She had to live with that monster."

"I don't know how she survived," Margie added, shaking her head.

Just then, Patricia was washing her hands at the sink when she suddenly froze, staring out the window. "I just saw someone go into Roy's house," she whispered, her voice trembling. "I think it's Roy."

Gail dropped the popcorn ball she was shaping, and they all rushed to the window. I joined them, my heart pounding. Sure enough, we saw a shadowy figure moving around inside the house.

"We need to call the sheriff," Gail said, grabbing her phone.

The tension was palpable as we waited for Sheriff Johnson to arrive. The women whispered among themselves, speculating about who it could be and what it meant. When the sheriff finally showed up, his face was grim.

He knocked on Roy's door, and after a moment, it opened to reveal Gary, looking nervous and sweaty.

"What are you doing here, Gary?" the sheriff asked, suspicion in his voice.

Gary stammered, "I-I was just looking for anything that might tell me where Roy went. He told me I could come by anytime."

The sheriff didn't look convinced. "You expect me to believe that?"

Gary's eyes darted around, and he looked like he was about to bolt. "I swear, Sheriff. Roy gave me permission."

The sheriff turned to me. "Loretta, is that true? Did Roy tell Gary he could come by anytime?"

I nodded slowly, remembering Roy's words. "Yes, Sheriff. Roy said Gary could come over whenever he needed to."

The sheriff still didn't seem convinced, but he sighed and stepped back. "Alright, Gary. But I'm keeping an eye on you."

Gary nodded quickly and almost ran out of the house. The sheriff watched him go, his face a mask of frustration.

"Something's not right here," he muttered to Gail. "But without proof, there's nothing I can do."

As the sheriff left, the unease settled over the house like a heavy blanket. The three women went back to making popcorn balls, but their chatter was subdued, and every little noise made us all jumpy.

Patricia glanced at me and tried to smile. "Loretta, how are you holding up?"

I shrugged, not really knowing how to answer. "I'm okay, I guess. Just scared."

Gail put a reassuring hand on my shoulder. "We're all scared, honey. But we're going to get through this. We just have to stick together."

They continued to talk, their voices low and serious, discussing theories and possibilities. Margie brought up the idea of forming a neighborhood watch, and they all agreed it was a good idea. They talked about how they could keep an eye on each other and make sure everyone was safe.

"I'm going to start locking my doors all the time," Patricia said firmly. "And I'm getting some extra locks put in, too."

Gail nodded. "I think we all should. We can't be too careful."

As the conversation continued, I could see the determination in their faces. They were scared, but they were also resolved to protect their families and their town.

It was strange to see the women I had always thought of as strong and invincible now looking so vulnerable.

~ 26 ~

HALLOWEEN NIGHT

It was finally Halloween night, and I didn't know whether to be excited or scared. Gail met her two friends, Patricia and Margie, at Bayou Bliss. Brenda, the owner, was dressed as a sexy devil, her red costume catching the light from the jack-o'-lanterns scattered around the coffee shop. We were waiting for my friends to join us. Jill arrived first, her witch's outfit rustling with every step. Tricia followed, looking fierce in her pirate attire, the toy sword at her side gleaming.

"You all look adorable. Here's a little treat to kick off your night," Brenda said with a grin, placing a small baggie of mixed candy in each of our bags.

"Thank you, Ms. Brenda," we chorused.

"We'll be at the town square," Gail said, her voice steady. "We'll be handing out popcorn balls, so come find us there when you're finished."

"Okay," I replied.

"And remember," Gail added firmly, "stick together, no matter what!"

We nodded and stepped out into the cool night. Our first stop was C&D Kwik Stop. Cindy and Dondi were dressed as zombies, their makeup eerily realistic.

"Trick or treat," we shouted.

"Eek... Look at those terrifying costumes!" Cindy exclaimed, pretending to shiver with fear.

We all burst into laughter.

"I think you all deserve some extra candy," Dondi said with a mischievous grin, slipping an extra candy bar into each of our bags. "You've outdone yourselves this year!"

"Thanks, Dondi!" Tricia said, eyeing her loot with excitement.

"Be careful out there," Cindy added, her tone more serious now. "Stick to the main street and stay where it's well-lit."

"We will!" I promised, glancing back as we headed out.

The streets were filled with trick-or-treaters, a whirlwind of laughter and shouts echoing through the night. Yet, amidst the colorful costumes, the clowns stood out, their garish smiles sending shivers down my spine.

"Too many clowns for my liking," I muttered, trying to shake off the unease that was settling in.

"Yeah, it's like they all decided to come as clowns tonight," Tricia said, her eyes scanning the crowd.

"Don't let them scare you," Jill added, though her voice wavered slightly.

Next, we headed to Shanster Travels. Shannon greeted us dressed as Batgirl, her cape billowing dramatically in the breeze. She flashed a wide smile and held out a bowl of candy. "Look at you all! These costumes are amazing!" she said, dropping a handful of treats into each of our bags.

"Thanks, Shannon!" Tricia grinned, already eyeing the candy.

But my attention was elsewhere. My heart skipped a beat as I spotted the clown from the hayfield, lurking near the entrance. I tugged at Jill's sleeve, panic tightening my chest.

"It's the same clown," I whispered, my voice trembling.

"Don't be silly," Jill replied, though I caught the flicker of unease in her eyes.

"Seriously, he's following us," I insisted, glancing back to where I'd seen him.

Jill stole a quick look over her shoulder, but the clown had already vanished into the shadows. "Let's just keep moving," she said, trying to sound confident. "He's probably just some guy trying to scare people."

"Well, he's doing a good job," I muttered, clutching my bag tighter and nervously scanning the darkness behind us. The night suddenly felt colder, the Halloween fun tainted by the chilling presence of the clown.

Shannon's cheerful voice cut through the tension. "You girls stay safe out there, okay?" she said, unaware of the fear creeping into our night.

"Thanks, we will," Jill replied, though her smile didn't reach her eyes.

As we walked away, I couldn't shake the feeling that the clown was still watching, lurking just out of sight. Every rustle in the breeze and shadowy corner felt like a threat, and I couldn't help but wonder if tonight's fun would turn into something much darker.

At Catrina's Closet, Catrina twirled in her princess costume, her tiara glittering under the streetlights. "You all look fabulous!" she said, handing out candy with a bright smile.

But my focus wasn't on the candy or Catrina's sparkling tiara. The clown was still there, trailing us at a distance, lurking just beyond the glow of the shop lights. When I pointed him out to Jill again, he seemed to notice and abruptly turned, walking the other way.

"See? He's just messing with us," Jill said, trying to brush it off, though her voice wavered slightly. It was clear she wasn't entirely convinced anymore.

"I don't like it," I muttered, my eyes constantly scanning the crowd for any sign of him. The way he seemed to disappear and reappear so effortlessly made my skin crawl.

Tricia looked between us, picking up on the tension. "What if he's more than just some guy playing a prank? What if he's really dangerous?"

"Don't start freaking out," Jill warned, though her tone was more uncertain than before. "Let's just stick to the plan—hit the last few stops and head back to the square."

But I couldn't shake the unease twisting in my gut. Every time we moved, it felt like the shadows moved with us, creeping closer. And no matter how hard I tried, I couldn't stop checking over my shoulder, half-expecting to see that eerie painted grin staring back at me from the darkness.

We made our way to the Library, where Lena was dressed as a pirate, much to Tricia's delight.

"Look, Ms. Lena! Matching outfits!" Tricia giggled, striking a dramatic pose as Terrie Lawson, the other librarian, snapped pictures.

Everyone was laughing and enjoying the moment, but I couldn't join in. My eyes kept darting around, scanning for any sign of the clown.

As we headed down the street, LaDonna stood in front of her bakery, dressed as a princess and cheerfully handing out bags of cookies. The table beside her showcased a cake shaped like a frog wearing a big gold crown, its eyes wide as if they were watching the crowd. Tricia couldn't resist running over to gush over the cake.

"Do you girls like my prince?" LaDonna asked with a playful grin.

We giggled, momentarily distracted from our fears.

"Here, have some cookies!" LaDonna said, smiling as she handed me a bag.

"Thanks," I replied, trying to force a smile, though the unease gnawed at me.

LaDonna's expression softened as she noticed my nervousness. "Everything okay?" she asked gently.

"Yeah, just... too many clowns tonight," I muttered, casting another quick glance over my shoulder.

LaDonna nodded, sensing my discomfort. "Well, stick close to your friends, and don't let anyone spoil your fun," she said, her voice reassuring.

I nodded, but as we moved on, the sense of being watched crept back in, stronger than ever. Even surrounded by lights and laughter, I couldn't shake the feeling that something was terribly wrong, and that sinister presence was still lurking in the shadows, waiting for its chance.

In the town square, the judge, the mayor, and a couple of older men sat on a bench, handing out candy to the children as they passed by. Gail and her friends were gathered at a table behind them, chatting and laughing, doing their best to keep things festive despite the unease that lingered in the air.

Micky stood outside his store, surrounded by a small group of concerned adults. He looked busy, his face grave as he talked with some of the parents of the missing women, nodding as they spoke in hushed tones.

"Let's go see Micky," Tricia suggested, her curiosity piqued.

"We'll come back later," Jill said, her eyes scanning the crowd, clearly distracted.

"Yeah, maybe when it's less crowded," I agreed, the knot of anxiety tightening in my chest.

But then I saw him—the clown—standing ahead of us, lingering near Tanya's Crawfish Shack. My heart raced as I pointed him out, but before anyone could get a good look, he disappeared into the shadows.

"Did you see that?" I asked, my voice rising in panic.

Jill and Tricia both looked, but by then, he was gone. "You're just spooking yourself," Tricia said, though I could tell she was trying to convince herself more than me.

"I'm telling you, he's following us," I insisted, my voice trembling. Every step we took seemed to bring him closer, as if he was toying with us, just waiting for the right moment.

Jill exchanged a nervous glance with Tricia. "Let's just get our candy and keep moving," she suggested, trying to sound calm.

Tanya greeted us warmly and handed each of us a small bag of candy. "Happy Halloween!" she said with a bright smile, playfully sweeping her cape behind her.

"I love your Little Red Riding Hood costume," Jill said with a grin.

"Thank you!" Tanya beamed, doing a little twirl.

I hesitated, then decided to speak up. "Ms. Tanya, I think someone's following us."

Her cheerful expression faded as concern crept in. "Who?" she asked, her voice softening.

"It's someone dressed as a clown," I explained, my eyes darting nervously around the square.

Tanya's gaze shifted in the direction I had been looking. "Would you like me to walk with you and help you find Gail?" she offered kindly.

I shook my head, still scanning the crowd. "No, it's okay. I don't see him now."

She nodded but leaned in closer, her voice serious. "Just be careful, alright? Stick together and don't go anywhere dark."

"We will," I promised.

As we stepped back outside, Jill glanced toward the other end of the square. "Should we go to the bar?"

"Why not?" Tricia replied, shrugging. "Last year, they gave us the most candy."

But even as they joked, I couldn't shake the growing sense of dread. The cheerful lights and laughter felt distant, like they couldn't reach me through the tension twisting in my gut. Every step toward the bar felt heavier, and I kept glancing over my shoulder, half-expecting that eerie clown to reappear at any moment.

As we approached the entrance to Jason's Bar, I noticed a flicker of movement out of the corner of my eye. My heart skipped a beat, but when I turned to look, there was nothing but shadows. "Let's just grab some candy and get back to the square quickly," I said, trying to hide the tremor in my voice.

"Agreed," Tricia said, her usual bravado noticeably absent.

The night was supposed to be fun, but the thrill of Halloween had twisted into something far more sinister, and I could tell I wasn't the only one feeling it. We huddled close together, trying to stay within the safety of the crowd, but even the cheerful laughter of other trick-or-treaters felt distant and hollow. The unsettling feeling of being followed by that horrid clown clung to me like a cold, invisible hand that refused to let go. Every flicker of movement in the shadows made my heart race, and I couldn't shake the fear that he was just waiting for the perfect moment to strike.

We walked into the bar, the dim lighting casting eerie shadows across the walls. Near the entrance stood another kid dressed in the same ghost outfit as mine, making my stomach twist with unease. Tricia and Jill rushed ahead, eagerly grabbing their candy from Jason.

"What are you waiting for? Go get your candy!" Tricia called out, her voice lighthearted.

But as I turned toward the counter, I noticed them walking out with the other ghost. My heart dropped. Panic surged through me, tightening in my chest. I bolted after them, fear clawing at my throat. But before I could reach the door, the clown stepped out of the shadows and blocked my path.

He was right in front of me, closer than ever before. The painted smile on his face was twisted into something grotesque, his eyes cold and menacing under the flickering streetlights. I froze, my blood running cold. Before I could scream, he lunged forward, grabbing me with an iron grip and covering my mouth with his gloved hand.

The stench of greasepaint and sweat filled my nostrils as I struggled against him, but he was strong—too strong. My muffled cries went unheard as he leaned in closer, his breath hot and foul against my ear.

"Shh," he hissed, his voice a sinister whisper that sent icy chills down my spine. I kicked and twisted, desperate to break free, but his grip was unyielding, like steel.

My pulse thundered in my ears as he dragged me back toward the shadows, away from the safety of the bar's lights. Every instinct screamed at me to fight, but fear paralyzed me, trapping me in his grasp. I could hear distant laughter and music from the square, but it felt miles away, as if I was slipping into some dark, isolated corner of the world.

In that moment, I realized this wasn't just some Halloween prank. This was real—and I was trapped in a nightmare with no escape in sight.

"You're coming with me," he snarled, his voice dripping with malice.

Desperation flooded through me—I had to do something, anything. Summoning every ounce of courage, I bit down hard on his hand. He let out a sharp hiss of pain, momentarily loosening his grip. It was enough. I screamed with all the force I could muster, hoping someone, anyone, would hear me.

But his reaction was swift and vicious. With a growl, he tore the ghost costume off me, the fabric ripping as it hit the ground in tatters. Before I could make another sound, he pressed a rag over my mouth and nose. The sharp, sickly sweet smell of chemicals filled my lungs, and I thrashed wildly, trying to resist. My vision blurred, the world tilting and spinning as darkness clawed at the edges of my consciousness.

"No..." I tried to scream, but the sound barely escaped my lips.

Everything faded to black, the sinister echo of the clown's laugh the last thing I heard before sinking into a cold, heavy darkness.

~ 27 ~

IS THIS A DREAM?

I woke up to the sound of a woman's voice, cheerful and lively, cutting through the eerie silence. "Loretta, it's time to cut the cake!" she called out.

"Mama?" I mumbled, rubbing my eyes and trying to shake the fog from my mind. As I looked around, confusion and disbelief washed over me.

I was back at the old campground—the place that had haunted my nightmares for years. Everything looked the same—the towering trees, the flickering firelight, and the small picnic table with the brightly decorated cake. Yet something about it all felt wrong, like I was trapped in a memory turned dark.

"What's wrong, sweetheart?" my mom asked, her voice soft and full of concern. She knelt beside me, her eyes crinkling with worry.

It felt so real, yet I knew it couldn't be, but how was I here now?

"How can this be?" I whispered, my eyes locking onto the cake in front of me. It was covered in colorful icing, with the words "Happy 4th Birthday, Loretta" spelled out in bright letters. The cheerful sight was a jarring contrast to the dread curling in my stomach.

I glanced around, taking in every detail. The sun was setting, casting a warm glow over everything, and the air was thick with the familiar smell of pine and smoke. Then it hit me like a punch to the gut—this was the day everything changed. This was the last time I saw my mom, the last moment of happiness before my world shattered.

Before I could say anything, Roy stumbled out from the woods, mumbling under his breath. "Thought an alligator was gonna get me," he grumbled, wiping his face with the back of his hand. "That piss took forever."

He reeked of alcohol, his words slurred and his movements unsteady as he staggered closer to the fire. Even in this twisted memory, he was just as I remembered—mean, drunk, and unpredictable.

My mom's smile wavered for just a second before she plastered it back on, trying to keep the mood light. "Let's sing 'Happy Birthday,'" she said, her voice a bit too cheerful, as if willing the darkness away. She started singing, her voice sweet and full of love, but the words felt hollow, like a desperate attempt to hold on to something that was slipping away.

Roy rolled his eyes and plopped down by the fire, ignoring the celebration. "You done yet?" he muttered, his gaze fixed on the flames.

"Come on, let's eat some cake," my mom said, cutting a big slice and handing it to me.

I sat next to her, savoring the sweetness of the cake and the warmth of her presence. For a fleeting moment, I felt safe, wrapped in the comfort of her love. But even as I clung to the happiness, a heavy sadness settled in my chest. I knew what was coming, and the dread of it gnawed at me.

Tears welled up in my eyes, blurring the colorful icing and the flickering firelight.

"Why are you crying, honey?" my mom asked, her voice soft as she wiped away my tears with her thumb.

"I miss you, Mama," I choked out, the words catching in my throat.

"Miss me? We're together every day, silly," she laughed, her eyes sparkling with that familiar joy I had held onto for years. "Hey, I have something to cheer you up. Open your present."

I unwrapped the gift with trembling hands, revealing a soft teddy bear with a blue butterfly embroidered on it.

"It's Mr. Teddy," I whispered, hugging the bear tightly. The warmth of the memory washed over me, filling me with a bittersweet sense of comfort.

"What are you going to call him?" she asked, her smile widening as she watched me cuddle the bear.

"I'll call him Mr. Teddy," I said, holding him close.

In that moment, I wanted to freeze time, to stay wrapped in the love and safety that only she could provide. The big gold locket she always wore shimmered in the firelight, catching my eye. The large 'C' engraved on the front stood out, a symbol of the bond we shared. Inside the locket was a picture of the two of us—her most cherished possession.

But then reality started to crack. "Can you put the little brat to bed so you and I can have some fun?" Roy sneered, his voice dripping with impatience. He leaned back in his chair, swigging from a half-empty bottle.

My mom's smile faltered, and fear flickered in her eyes. "Come on, sweetie, let's get you to bed," she said softly, her voice strained.

She led me to the tent and tucked me and Mr. Teddy into the sleeping bag, her hands trembling slightly as she kissed my forehead. Then, in a voice that wavered with hidden tears, she whispered, "I love you," and gave me a butterfly kiss, her eyelashes fluttering against my cheek.

"I love you too, Mom," I whispered back, clinging to the sound of her voice.

I lay there, the comfort of Mr. Teddy doing little to ease the growing sense of dread. The warmth of the fire outside dimmed, replaced by the chill of fear. Just as I was about to drift off, the silence was shattered by my mom's scream—a sound so filled with terror that it jolted me upright. My heart pounded in my chest as I peeped out of the tent.

What I saw froze the blood in my veins. Roy was on top of her, his face twisted in rage as he struck her again and again.

"Stop it, Roy!" she cried, but her pleas only seemed to fuel his anger.

He grabbed a heavy log from the firewood pile and swung it at her head. The sickening sound of the impact echoed through the trees, and blood sprayed across the ground.

I clamped my hand over my mouth, trying to stifle the sobs that threatened to escape. I couldn't look away as Roy continued to bludgeon her, the warmth of her love replaced by the cold, unforgiving reality of death. Her body went limp, lifeless, but he didn't stop. He kept hitting her until there was nothing left but blood and broken bones.

When he finally stopped, he stood there panting, his eyes wild with fear and realization. He looked around like a trapped animal, his gaze darting to the darkness of the woods. Then, with a desperate urgency, he grabbed a shovel from his truck and started digging a grave at the edge of the clearing. The sound of the shovel scraping against the dirt was deafening, each thrust into the ground a brutal reminder of what I had just witnessed.

I wanted to scream, to run, to wake up from this nightmare, but I was paralyzed, my body refusing to move. All I could do was watch as he tossed her lifeless body into the shallow grave and began covering it with dirt. With each shovel full of earth, the love and warmth that had filled my heart minutes ago was buried alongside her.

Tears streamed down my face as I clutched Mr. Teddy tighter, trying to find some comfort in his soft fur. But all I could feel was the icy grip of fear, wrapping itself around my heart. The horror of that night would never leave me—it was seared into my soul, a wound that would never heal.

And as Roy stood there, staring at the freshly covered grave, he mumbled to himself, "No one will ever find you." His voice was cold, detached, as if he had buried not just her body, but every last trace of the woman who had once been my world.

I curled up tighter in my sleeping bag, praying that this nightmare would end, but deep down, I knew it wouldn't. This was my reality—a memory that would haunt me forever, a moment frozen in time that I could never escape.

~ 28 ~

I REMEMBER!

"Loretta!" A woman's scream pierced the darkness, yanking me out of unconsciousness. My eyes fluttered open, and I found myself engulfed in shadows, my heart thundering like it was trying to break free from my chest.

"Loretta!" This time, it was Micky's voice—his English accent sharp with panic and desperation.

"Over here!" I choked out, my voice trembling, raw from fear and dryness.

Suddenly, Gail, Micky, and the sheriff burst through the trees, their flashlights slicing through the dark. The beams landed on me, and their faces came into view—etched with pure, raw concern, breaths ragged from their frantic search.

"Oh my God! Are you okay? What happened?" they cried, their voices tumbling over one another in a rush of relief, panic, and desperate worry.

"The clown... he grabbed me," I sobbed, throwing myself into Gail's arms, clinging to her like she was my only anchor in a storm. My body shook uncontrollably, wracked with fear. "And... I remember. I remember what happened to my mom. Roy... Roy killed her and buried her right there." My trembling hand lifted, pointing into the darkness between the trees.

The words tore out of me in broken pieces, the memories crashing back like waves, drowning me in a mix of horror and grief. The terror of the present collided with the buried trauma of the past, and all I could do was cling to Gail, shaking and crying as the truth clawed its way out of me.

The deputies sprang into action, their flashlights stabbing through the dark, cutting across tangled branches as they combed the area for Roy. The beams danced over the dense underbrush, turning every rustle into a potential threat. The sheriff knelt beside me, his usual stern expression softened by worry. His voice was low, almost soothing, like he was trying not to startle a wild animal.

"How did you find me?" I managed to whisper, my voice small and shaky.

"Thanks to Micky," the sheriff said, glancing over at him. "He knew exactly where you'd be. I'll admit, he's earned another believer in his psychic skills tonight."

"Thank you, Micky," I said, my words cracking as I threw myself into his arms. His embrace was strong, steady, like he was holding me together while everything else around me felt like it was falling apart.

Before I could fully catch my breath, a shout sliced through the night like a blade.

"Sheriff, come here, quick!" one of the deputies hollered from the edge of the swamp, his voice sharp with urgency.

The sheriff took off running, and I followed on shaky legs, my pulse pounding in my ears. The air was thick with tension, every sound amplified in the silence. When we reached the edge of the swamp, my breath caught in my throat.

There, half-submerged in the muddy water, was a man lying face down. The deputies, moving cautiously, flipped him over. The scene that greeted us was like something out of a nightmare—his body was torn apart, covered in jagged gashes, his clothes shredded and soaked in blood.

"It looks like an alligator got him," the deputy muttered, his voice strained with grim disbelief.

But I couldn't focus on his words—my breath froze in my lungs as I recognized the face beneath the blood and grime. It was Gary. A wave of confusion and fear crashed over me, memories I'd buried suddenly tearing through my mind with ruthless clarity.

I staggered back, my body trembling as panic gripped me. The events of that night, buried deep for so long, now resurfaced, bringing with them a terror I'd hoped was lost to time.

Nearby, the deputies discovered Roy's truck, partially hidden in the brush, its presence like a shadow looming over the scene. The sight of it sent a jolt of dread through me—this was where everything had unraveled, where my life had been shattered.

The sheriff's voice was gentle but firm as he pulled me aside. "Loretta, can you show us where Roy buried your mom?"

My heart pounded wildly, each beat echoing the terror of that night. I nodded, though fear made every step feel like wading through thick, suffocating mud. As I led them deeper into the woods, the memories clawed their way back, vivid and cruel. I could almost hear my mom's laughter, see the glow of the fire—before it all turned into a nightmare. I remembered Roy's twisted grin as he buried her, the coldness in his eyes, and the helplessness that paralyzed me as I watched from the shadows.

The deputies began to dig, their shovels cutting through the earth with grim purpose. Each strike sent a shiver through me, the sound echoing the hollow thud of my heart. The tension was unbearable, tightening with every shovelful of dirt that was moved. My breaths came in ragged gasps as I clutched Gail's hand, barely holding myself together.

Then, they hit something solid. The digging slowed, and with agonizing care, they uncovered what was left of her. My mom's remains lay there, a tragic confirmation of what I'd always known deep down but never wanted to face.

Tears poured down my face as I collapsed to my knees, overwhelmed by a flood of grief and twisted relief. She was finally found, but the cost was more than I could bear. The agony of that night, buried for years, was suddenly raw and fresh again.

But even as I cried, a deeper, more chilling realization took hold. This was only part of the nightmare. Roy was still out there, and with every haunting memory resurfacing, I knew that the darkness that had taken root in our town wasn't gone. It was still watching, waiting for its next move.

The sheriff's voice sounded distant, like it was miles away, as he called for the team to search the area. But I barely heard him—my mind was lost in the swirling storm of memories and fear. The nightmare wasn't over. Not yet.

A few minutes later, one of the deputies hurried over to the sheriff, holding a crumpled note he'd pulled from Gary's pocket. The paper was smeared with dirt and blood, its edges torn, as if it had been clutched tightly in a moment of desperation. The sheriff's eyes narrowed as he took it, carefully unfolding it. His expression grew more serious with each passing second as he scanned the words, then he looked at me with an intensity that made my heart race.

"Loretta," he said softly, his voice careful and measured, "this letter is for you. Do you want me to read it?"

I shook my head quickly, fear gripping my chest, but something inside me knew I needed to hear it. The sheriff took a deep breath, his eyes never leaving mine, and began to read aloud:

"Dearest Loretta,

I'm so sorry I didn't step forward sooner. For years, I've stayed in the shadows, watching over you from a distance, always nearby, always keeping an eye on you. I had to protect you from Roy. You may have wondered why I always seemed to be lurking, never too far away. It was to make sure you were safe, to do what little I could to shield you from the horrors he brought into your life.

Seeing how Roy treated you, how he tormented you, ripped me apart inside. I couldn't stay silent any longer. I knew it was time to act, even if it meant revealing the truth I've kept hidden all these years.

Loretta, I am your dad. I've loved you from afar, but I can no longer hide in the shadows. You deserve to know the truth and to have the love and protection that's always been yours.

With all my love, Gary (your dad)"

The words hung in the air like a dense fog, each one hitting me like a punch to the gut. My breath caught in my throat as the realization crashed over me. Gary... was my father? The man I never liked, who always seemed to be hanging around because of his friendship with Roy—he wasn't just some unwanted presence. He had been watching over me, trying to protect me from Roy's darkness.

A tidal wave of emotions surged through me—anger, confusion, sorrow, and a strange, aching relief. My mind spun as I tried to piece it all together, the weight of the truth settling over me like a suffocating blanket. How many times had I looked over my shoulder, only to see him watching? How many times had I misjudged him, thinking he was just another threat in the shadows?

The sheriff's voice broke through the whirlwind in my head. "I know this is a lot, Loretta. Take your time."

But I couldn't answer. I just stared at the note, trying to reconcile the horror of everything that had happened with the reality that Gary—my dad—had been there all along, fighting his own demons to keep me safe. The world felt upside down, every truth I'd known shattered and replaced with something darker, more twisted, and deeply unsettling.

The night's chill tightened around me, and the shadows seemed to creep closer, whispering that the horrors of the past were still alive, still hungry. The monsters weren't gone—they were just waiting, lurking in the darkness. This revelation was another twisted piece in a puzzle that kept growing more sinister. The truth had clawed its way into the light, but instead of bringing comfort, it only made the fear more real, leaving me dreading what fresh nightmare might strike next.

A deputy rushed over, handing the sheriff a small wooden box. "We found this near Gary's body," he said, his voice low.

Gail's face went pale, and she gasped. "Oh my God! That's just like the box someone sent me and Loretta!"

The sheriff's eyes darkened as he carefully opened the box. Inside was a single note, the words scrawled in sharp, jagged handwriting: 'TICK TOCK.'

The sheriff's jaw clenched, his voice a low, tense whisper. "That doesn't add up. Was he the one behind the note?"

A shiver raced down my spine as I met Gail's eyes. Her fear mirrored mine, and for a moment, it felt like the ground beneath us could crumble at any second.

It's a chilling realization I can't piece together. I whisper to myself, *Why would Gary send me the 'Tick Tock' note?* The thought gnaws at me, making no sense. *He was protecting me, not trying to scare me.*

Gail must sense the confusion churning inside me because she gently places a hand on my shoulder. "We don't know for sure it was Gary, sweetheart," she says softly.

Micky watches me carefully, his eyes narrowing in thought. "Gary's not the type to send threats, especially to you," he mutters. "But someone out there wants you and Gail rattled."

"But who?" I ask, the question hanging in the air like a cold weight.

Micky shrugs, the worry clear in his expression. "That's the real question, isn't it?"

The sheriff placed a reassuring hand on my shoulder, his gaze steady but laced with urgency. "We'll get to the bottom of this, Loretta," he said, but even in his calm tone, I could hear the underlying tension.

Gail pulled me into a tight hug, her warmth the only thing holding back the cold fear creeping up my skin. I clung to her, trying to block out the dread swirling around us.

The nightmare wasn't over. If anything, it was just beginning, and the truth that had finally surfaced only brought with it more darkness.

As the deputies continued their search, Micky quietly built a fire. The flames flickered and danced, casting eerie shadows that seemed to twist and morph into the ghosts of my past. I sat between Micky and Gail, clutching their hands as if they were lifelines. Every crackle of the fire, every flicker of light, seemed to whisper pieces of the story that had been buried for so long. The pieces were starting to fit together, but the picture they formed was darker and more tragic than I could have imagined.

The sheriff's team worked tirelessly, their determination slicing through the tension hanging in the air. Every rustle of leaves, every snap of a twig, sent my heart racing. The swampy forest, once the source of all my childhood fears, had now become the stage where long-buried truths were being dragged into the light. It felt like we were fighting not just for answers, but for justice, for closure—for a way to finally put the nightmare to rest.

"Loretta," Micky said softly, his voice like a warm blanket against the chill in the air. He squeezed my hand gently. "We'll make sure Roy never hurts you or anyone else again."

I nodded, swallowing the lump in my throat as anger and sorrow twisted inside me. My mom's face, her warm laughter, the way she used to hold me tight—all those memories flashed before my eyes, sharper and more painful than ever. The ache of missing her was almost unbearable.

Hours passed, but the search pressed on. The deputies uncovered more clues, each one a piece of the twisted story of Roy and Gary. The realization that Gary had been trying to protect me all along, driven by a love I hadn't known, was a mix of bitter and sweet. I'd spent so long resenting him, not realizing he was silently watching over me, sacrificing everything in his own way.

As the first light of dawn began to stretch across the swamp, the darkness started to lift, chased away by the creeping rays of the sun. The sheriff approached, his face lined with exhaustion but still carrying that determined resolve.

"Loretta," he said, his voice gentle but firm, "I know you're tired, but we need you to come with us to the station. There's a lot we have to go over, but I promise you, we'll get to the bottom of this."

I nodded, feeling a lump in my throat as Gail wrapped me in a hug.

My life, all the repressed memories, came to light. Everything I thought I knew had been turned upside down. My monster was still on the loose. I knew he was out there, lurking, waiting to finish what he started. And as I stood there, trembling, one thing was clear—nothing would ever be the same again.

~ 29 ~

THE MISSING TEACHER

As we drove back into town, the morning sun rose, bathing everything in a warm, golden light. It felt as if the sun itself was reassuring me that everything would be alright. Despite not finding Roy, his dark secret had been unearthed. After Micky found me last night, I dared to hope that things might finally settle down. However, the sight of the crowd gathered outside the sheriff's office told me otherwise.

As we pulled up, an older woman was standing with Mrs. Staggs, her cries piercing the morning air. I felt a pang in my heart, knowing all too well the fear and pain she was feeling.

The sheriff stepped forward, his face somber. "What's going on here, Mrs. Staggs?" he asked, his eyes on the distressed woman.

Mrs. Staggs placed a comforting hand on the woman's shoulder. "Sheriff, this is Mrs. Lopez. Her daughter, Sophia, went missing last night. She didn't come home."

Mrs. Lopez's cries became more frantic. "Please, you have to find her! She went to pick up dinner at Tanya's Crawfish and never came back. She would never just disappear like this!"

The sheriff nodded, his face grave. "We'll do everything in our power, ma'am. Did she mention anything out of the ordinary? Any new faces she might've encountered or someone she seemed wary of?"

Mrs. Lopez shook her head vigorously. "No, she just said she was going to get dinner. She doesn't have any enemies. She's a teacher, for God's sake!"

The sheriff frowned, his gaze turning thoughtful. "Did she have any reason to go to Jason's Bar?"

The question seemed to shock Mrs. Lopez. She pulled back, her eyes wide with anger. "No! Sophia doesn't drink. She wouldn't go to a place like that. How dare you suggest such a thing!"

The sheriff raised his hands, trying to calm her. "I'm sorry, ma'am. I had to ask. All the other women who've gone missing were last seen at Jason's Bar. We're trying to find any connection we can."

Micky stepped forward, his voice gentle and reassuring. "Mrs. Lopez, I know this is incredibly difficult for you. Let's step inside so you can have a private conversation with the sheriff, alright?"

Mrs. Lopez looked at Micky, her anger melting into despair. She nodded weakly, allowing him to guide her inside. "I know you," she said, her voice trembling. "You're the man everyone talks about, the one who can speak to the dead."

Micky gave her a reassuring smile.

"Can you hear my daughter?" she asked, her voice breaking. "If you can, my worst fears are true."

Micky shook his head slightly. "No, Mrs. Lopez, I can't."

Relief washed over her face, and she managed a gentle smile.

I sat huddled in the corner of the sheriff's office, hugging my knees to my chest. Everything still felt like a bad dream, but I couldn't stop watching. Mrs. Lopez was sitting across from the sheriff, twisting a handkerchief in her hands like she was trying to wring out all the fear inside her. The sheriff's face was serious, and even though his voice was calm, I could tell he was worried too.

Micky stood nearby, always calm and steady, and he'd glance at me every so often, giving me a small, reassuring smile. I tried to smile back, but I couldn't. I was too caught up in listening to what they were saying, trying to piece together the fear I felt swirling in the room. I wished I could close my ears and block it all out, but I needed to know what was going on, even if just hearing it made my heart pound like it was trying to break free. After all, *my* monster was behind all of this.

"Mrs. Lopez, I need to ask a few more questions," the sheriff said gently. "Did Sophia mention anyone who might have been bothering her? Any unusual behavior lately?"

Mrs. Lopez shook her head, tears streaming down her face. "No, she was just her usual self. Always kind, always caring. She loved her students. She was looking forward to the school year."

I watched as Micky tried to comfort her, his voice low and soothing. He glanced at me, and I knew what he was thinking. This was just like all the other cases. Another woman taken, another family torn apart.

"Do you remember what time she arrived at Tanya's Crawfish Shack?" the sheriff asked.

"Around seven o'clock," Mrs. Lopez sniffled, trying to hold back her tears.

The sheriff, looking puzzled, glanced over at Micky. "What time did the girls tell you about Loretta?"

"Right around that time," Micky confirmed.

"Mrs. Lopez," the sheriff said, standing and gently taking her hand. "Could you please have a seat in the lobby for a moment?"

She slowly stood up, and Micky gently guided her to a chair just outside the office.

The sheriff stood at the door and motioned for me to stay inside.

"Loretta," he said softly, "I know you're tired, and you've been through a lot, so I'll make this as quick as possible." He pulled out the chair across from me and took a seat, leaning in slightly with that serious look he always had when something important was about to be said.

"I'm okay, Sheriff," I tried to smile, but it felt forced.

"Do you think the clown who grabbed you was Gary?" he asked gently.

I shook my head, feeling my heart pound in my chest. "No, I don't think it was him. It was someone else." I hesitated, my voice trembling as I asked the question that had been gnawing at me. "Do you think Gary is my father?"

The sheriff's expression softened. "We'll definitely run some tests and let you know," he said, offering a reassuring smile that didn't quite reach his eyes.

I nodded slowly and lowered my head, a sick feeling swirling in my stomach. The weight of everything felt like it was pressing down on me, making it hard to breathe. I wasn't sure if I wanted the answer or if knowing would just make everything worse.

"Did the person who grabbed you say anything to you?" the sheriff asked, his eyes searching mine intently.

I swallowed hard, the memory just out of reach. "Yes, but... I was so scared. I don't remember what he said."

"Did you recognize the voice?" the sheriff asked gently, leaning in closer, his tone urging me to dig deeper into my memories.

I opened my mouth to respond, but before I could answer, the door flew open and Patricia and Margie burst into the office, their faces flooded with relief the moment they saw me.

"Oh, thank goodness, Loretta!" Patricia cried as she rushed over and pulled me into a tight hug. "We were so worried about you."

Margie quickly joined in, wrapping her arms around us both. Her hug was warm and reassuring, and I felt a tear slip down my cheek. "We're so glad Micky found you. We've been scared out of our minds," Margie added, her voice shaky with emotion.

I clung to them, feeling the warmth of their love. It was a small comfort in the midst of all this chaos.

The sheriff cleared his throat gently, drawing our attention. He gave me a soft, understanding look. "Loretta, you've been through more than anyone should ever have to. You've been thorough enough, and I'm so sorry about everything that's happened to you." His voice was full of sincerity, the kind that made me believe he really meant it.

I nodded, a lump forming in my throat, and managed a weak, "Thank you, Sheriff."

He gave me a small, reassuring smile before stepping out of the office. As soon as he opened the door, the noise from outside crashed into the room. Cameras flashed, and reporters shouted questions, desperate for answers. The sheriff's face turned stern as he stepped into the chaos.

Gail took my hand, squeezing it gently. "Come on, sweetheart," she said softly, guiding me to the door. Her two friends, Patricia and Margie, followed close behind as we stood just inside, watching the scene unfold.

"Is Gary the serial killer?" one reporter shouted, pushing forward.

The sheriff shook his head firmly. "We don't know at this time. We're investigating all leads."

"What about Roy?" another voice demanded. "Is he involved?"

The sheriff's expression remained steady. "We can't say at this time. We're doing everything we can to find out."

The crowd's murmuring grew louder, voices blending into a mix of fear and anger. "Roy is a murderer!" someone yelled. "He killed Loretta's mother!"

"Did he kill Gary?" another person hollered. "Gary was a good man!"

The sheriff raised his hands, trying to calm the escalating tension. "Please, everyone, we're doing our best. We need your cooperation and patience."

Despite his attempts, the town was in an uproar. They were relieved I'd been found, but the anger toward Roy was thick in the air, nearly tangible. They already knew about Mama's body being discovered, and now they were out for blood. I could see it in their eyes—they wanted justice, and they wanted it fast.

Standing there in the doorway, I could feel the weight of all their emotions pressing down on me. It was overwhelming, and I squeezed Gail's hand a little tighter, grateful she was there.

The sheriff walked back inside, his expression grim as one of his deputies hurried over. "What are we going to do?" the deputy asked, his voice edged with concern.

"They're angry," the sheriff replied, glancing toward the door where the crowd's angry murmurs still filtered through. "And they have every right to be. But we need to take control of this before we have a vigilante situation on our hands."

Inside, Micky continued to comfort Mrs. Lopez. "We'll find Sophia," he promised, his eyes steady. "We won't stop until we do."

Mrs. Lopez nodded, clinging to those words, though her eyes were a mix of hope and fear. "Please, just find her. She's all I have."

The sheriff quickly gathered his deputies, his tone all business. "We need to comb through every inch of this town," he ordered, the authority in his voice unmistakable. "No stone unturned. We need everyone on this—nobody rests until we find something."

"Can we help?" Gail asked.

The sheriff nodded. "Yes, absolutely. The more eyes we have, the better our chances of finding Sophia. We'll set up search grids. I'll have someone coordinate volunteers."

Patricia and Margie both nodded, ready to pitch in without hesitation.

Micky looked at me, his eyes filled with determination. "Loretta, you'll stay with me at the store. It's safer there."

I nodded, my heart racing, trusting him completely. The weight of everything happening around us made it hard to think straight, but Micky's calm, steady voice helped ground me.

As the sheriff organized the search party, Micky and I slipped out quietly and headed toward his store, Micky's Magical Things. The moment we stepped inside, the familiar scent of old books and warm incense washed over me. The outside world felt distant, and for a moment, the store felt like a sanctuary, a place where the darkness couldn't touch us.

The town was rallying together, determined to find Sophia, and that sense of unity sparked a flicker of hope inside me. The fear was still there, but it wasn't as paralyzing with Micky by my side. As I looked around the shop, surrounded by the comforting clutter of trinkets and mysteries, I knew that whatever happened next, this day would be a turning point for all of us—one we'd never forget.

~ 30 ~

SHE'S HERE!

Micky closed the door behind us, his eyes softening as he looked at me. "Loretta, I know this is all a lot to handle. But you're strong, stronger than you realize."

I glanced around the shop, taking in the cozy clutter of crystals, old books, and trinkets that filled every nook and cranny. The familiar sight eased the tension in my chest, and for the first time that day, I felt a bit of calm wash over me. "I know, Micky. I just... I just want this all to be over."

Micky smiled gently, his eyes full of understanding. "I know. And it will be." He paused and reached into his pocket, pulling out a small, shimmering stone. It looked almost otherworldly, with milky hues streaked with soft blues, pinks, and lavender, catching the light in a way that made it seem alive. "I have something for you, Loretta. Your wishing stone has fulfilled its purpose, and it's time to replace it with this."

I stared at the stone, mesmerized by its soft, ethereal glow. "What is it?" I asked, my voice barely above a whisper.

Micky handed it to me, his eyes sparkling with a hint of mystery. "It's another wishing stone, but this one is special. With it, you can communicate with your mom. It also carries a message from her—she wanted you to have it."

I clutched the stone, feeling a gentle warmth spread through my hand. "A message?"

Micky nodded, his eyes kind and encouraging. "Close your eyes, Loretta. Picture your mom."

I did as he said, closing my eyes and letting my thoughts drift back to memories of her. I could see her warm smile, feel her gentle touch, and remember how she used to give me butterfly kisses before bed. The memories were bittersweet, filling me with both love and an aching sense of loss.

As I focused on those memories, the stone in my hand grew warmer, and suddenly, I felt a presence—a comforting, familiar presence that wrapped around me like a soft embrace. "Mama?" I whispered, tears prickling at the corners of my eyes.

In my mind, I saw her, standing there with her arms open wide, just like she used to when I was little. "Loretta, my sweet girl," she said, her voice soft and full of love. "You're so brave. I'm so proud of you."

Tears streamed down my face as I reached out, desperate to hold her, to feel her warmth just one more time.

"I miss you, Mama," I choked out, my heart aching with the words.

"I know, sweetheart," she said, her image flickering like a candle in the wind, delicate but real. "But I'm always with you. You carry my love in your heart, and that's something no one can ever take away. Stay strong, my brave girl. I love you."

The warmth of the stone slowly faded, and as it did, her image began to blur, slipping away like a dream. I opened my eyes, blinking back the tears, my heart swelling with a mix of love and longing.

"Thank you, Micky," I whispered, clutching the stone to my chest, holding onto that precious moment.

Micky placed a comforting hand on my shoulder, his expression full of understanding. "Your mama's always with you, Loretta. Don't ever forget that."

Without thinking, I hugged Micky tightly, feeling a wave of gratitude and comfort. In a world that felt so scary and uncertain, this moment of connection, this reminder of my mama's love, was exactly what I needed to keep going.

"Let me get a chain for your new wishing stone," he said, heading behind the counter. After a moment, he returned with a delicate, sparkly silver chain that glinted in the soft light of the shop. "Now, anytime you want to talk to your mom or make a wish, just do what you did before."

Micky carefully threaded the stone onto the chain, its shimmering hues catching the light as it dangled between his fingers. He leaned in and gently placed the necklace around my neck, securing the clasp. The stone rested just above my heart, its warmth seeping into my skin.

"There you go," he said, stepping back and smiling warmly. "It's close to your heart, where it belongs. Remember, whenever you need her, she's just a wish away."

I touched the stone, feeling its comforting presence and the connection it held to my mama. "Thank you, Micky," I whispered. The weight of the stone was light, but it felt like it carried so much more—hope, love, and the strength to keep going, no matter what came next.

We spent the rest of the morning in the shop, the tension of the search outside hanging over us like a cloud. Micky tried to keep things light, offering me snacks and distracting me with stories, but it was hard to ignore the worry gnawing at my insides.

As the hours passed, news began to trickle in from the search parties. They hadn't found Sophia yet, but the town wasn't giving up. People were searching everywhere—through fields, down alleyways, in abandoned buildings—leaving no stone unturned.

Micky and I waited in the shop, the minutes dragging into what felt like endless hours. The ticking of the old clock on the wall grew louder, each second stretching out longer than the last. Every time someone walked by outside, I found myself glancing at the door, half hoping and half dreading that someone might burst in with news—good or bad.

Finally, the door creaked open, and Gail stepped inside, her face etched with exhaustion and worry. Her shoulders sagged as she took a deep breath, brushing stray hair from her face. "Any news?" she asked, her voice raspy and tired.

Micky shook his head. "Not yet."

Gail's eyes briefly closed, as if she was summoning the strength to keep going. "The whole town's out there looking, turning over every rock and chasing every lead. We're not giving up until we find her."

She walked over and sat beside me, placing a comforting hand on my back. "How are you holding up, sweetie?"

"I'm okay," I whispered, though the knot in my stomach told a different story. "I just want them to find her."

Gail gave me a small, tired smile. "We all do. And we will."

I nodded, holding onto that fragile hope like a lifeline. The whole town was united in its efforts, and I had to believe we would bring Sophia home and finally find Roy. We couldn't give up—not now.

As the sun began to set, the door creaked open, and the sheriff stepped inside. His face was drawn and tired, shadows under his eyes. "We haven't found her yet," he said, his voice heavy with frustration, "but we're not giving up. The search will continue through the night if necessary."

Gail nodded beside me, her grip on my shoulder tightening. I could feel her worry through the way her fingers pressed into my skin.

Before the silence could settle back in, the bell above the door chimed, and Patricia and Margie rushed in, their faces flushed with urgency.

"Sheriff," Patricia panted, trying to catch her breath, "we found Sophia's car near the old mill."

My heart leaped into my throat. The old mill. The place where we had uncovered the hidden room, where so many secrets had been buried. My mind raced with fear —what if the old mill was where Sophia had been taken? What if we were too late?

"Any sign of Sophia?" the sheriff asked, his voice edged with urgency as he turned toward Margie.

Margie shook her head, her expression heavy with worry. "Just her car. The search party is focusing all their efforts there now."

The sheriff's jaw tightened, and he rushed to the door. "We need to go. Now!"

Micky, Patricia, and Margie exchanged determined looks and nodded, quickly grabbing their things. I barely had time to process what was happening before Gail took my hand, her grip firm and protective. "Stay close to me, Loretta," she said, her voice steady but laced with concern.

As we hurried toward the old mill, the town was buzzing with activity. People lined the streets, some joining the search while others offered supplies or simply watched in anxious anticipation. The mill, its dark history casting a long shadow over Bayou Vista, loomed ahead like a ghost from the past. Its silhouette stood stark against the twilight sky, a grim reminder of the secrets it held.

When we arrived, the scene was tense and chaotic. Flashlights cut through the growing darkness, beams of light sweeping across the overgrown grounds and crumbling walls. Voices echoed as people called out Sophia's name, each shout filled with desperation and hope.

The sheriff and Micky immediately took charge, their focus razor-sharp. "We need to split into teams and cover every inch of this place," the sheriff barked, pointing out sections of the mill and surrounding woods. Micky nodded, his calm demeanor steadying everyone around him, even as the tension crackled in the air.

I stuck close to Gail. My heart raced as we moved closer to the old mill's entrance, the memories of what we'd uncovered there still fresh in my mind.

As the search intensified, I clutched the stone around my neck, silently wishing for Sophia's safety, praying we weren't too late.

Suddenly, a shout pierced the tense night air. "Over here! I found something!"

Everyone turned toward the voice, and within seconds, flashlights converged on a small area near the mill's entrance. We all rushed over, hearts pounding with a mix of hope and dread. One of the searchers stood there, holding up a torn piece of fabric, its edges frayed and dirty. "It's a part of her dress," he said, his voice trembling.

The sheriff took the fabric, examining it closely under the beam of his flashlight. "We're on the right track," he said. "Spread out and search the area thoroughly. Don't miss a thing."

The search party quickly fanned out, combing the ground with renewed vigor. Flashlights bobbed in the darkness, illuminating every shadow, every patch of ground where a clue might be hidden. Every rustle of leaves, every snap of a twig had us on edge, nerves wound tight like a coiled spring.

I stayed close to Gail, my heart racing with each step. The cold breeze seemed to carry whispers, twisting through the trees like ghostly fingers. The old mill loomed above us, its dark windows staring down like empty eyes, holding secrets we were desperate to uncover.

Micky, ever vigilant, his eyes scanning the ground and the mill's crumbling walls. "Stay sharp," he murmured to the others as they pressed forward. "She could be close."

The night felt endless, the seconds dragging into what felt like hours. The hope that had sparked with the discovery of the fabric was now mingled with fear—fear that we might be too late, fear of what we might find.

Then, in the stillness of the night, we heard it—a faint, desperate cry for help. "Help! Please, help me!"

The sound sent a jolt through the entire search party, spurring everyone into frantic action. Flashlights whipped toward the direction of the voice, and we moved as one, hearts pounding with a mix of fear and hope. The cry was faint, but it was there—alive and pleading.

"Over here!" the sheriff barked, leading the charge as we pushed through the overgrown bushes and brambles near the back of the mill. The beam of his flashlight cut through the darkness, guiding us as we followed the faint, trembling voice.

Then we saw her—hidden among the dense underbrush, tied to a tree. Sophia. Her clothes were torn, her face streaked with dirt and tears, but she was alive. The sight of her sent a wave of relief crashing over us all.

The sheriff and Micky rushed forward, quickly working to untie the ropes binding her to the tree. "It's okay, you're safe now," Micky murmured, his voice soft as he gently freed her. Sophia's body shook with sobs as she collapsed into their arms, her fear and exhaustion pouring out after what must have felt like an eternity of terror.

As the sheriff called in the good news on his radio, the rest of the search party gathered around, offering comforting words and blankets. I could see the strength return to Sophia's eyes as she clung to the people who had come to save her.

Gail squeezed my hand, her eyes shining with tears of relief. I could feel the tension in the air begin to melt away, replaced by a warmth that spread through the crowd as everyone realized we had found her.

Sophia's mother, who had been waiting anxiously with Mrs. Staggs, rushed forward the moment she saw her daughter, enveloping her in a tearful embrace. "Thank God you're safe," she cried, her voice breaking with emotion. "I was so worried."

Sophia clung to her mother, her sobs of relief mingling with the cheers and shouts of the townspeople.

"Sophia," the sheriff asked gently, though his voice carried the weight of urgency, "did you see who took you?"

She shook her head, her eyes wide and haunted. "No, I didn't see his face. He kept it covered the whole time."

The sheriff nodded, his expression grim, but understanding. Before he could ask more, one of the deputies approached. "Should we keep combing the area for Roy?" he asked, his voice laced with tension.

The sheriff sighed, scanning the dark woods surrounding the mill. "He's probably long gone by now. We'll resume the search at first light tomorrow morning. Let everyone get some rest—we're not done yet."

As the search party began to disperse, families and neighbors sharing hugs and words of comfort, Gail wrapped me in a tight embrace. "We did it, Loretta. We found her."

I nodded, unable to hold back the tears that flowed freely down my face. It felt like a weight had lifted, but there was still a knot of fear in my chest. Roy was still out there, and as much as this victory mattered, the darkness hadn't fully passed.

Micky approached, his eyes filled with pride and relief. "I'm so glad she's safe," he said softly.

I clutched the wishing stone hanging around my neck, feeling its comforting warmth and the love it represented. "Me too, Micky. Me too."

Once filled with fear and uncertainty, the night was now glowing with a renewed hope. The terror that had gripped Bayou Vista was beginning to ease, replaced by the strength and unity of our community. We had come together, and that shared determination had made all the difference.

I looked up at the night sky, the stars twinkling against the velvet darkness. "Mama, we did it. We found her," I whispered.

The stars seemed to shimmer brighter, as if answering me, and I smiled, knowing in my heart that my mama was with me, watching over us all.

The magic of Bayou Vista wasn't just in the wishing stones or the mysteries surrounding us; it was alive in the bonds we shared and the love that held us together.

~ 31 ~

THE MORNING AFTER

The aroma of pancakes wafted through the air as I made my way to the kitchen, guided by the delicious scent. Gail stood at the stove, skillfully flipping a golden stack of pancakes. The table was already set, and a bowl of fresh strawberries and a can of whipped cream awaited.

"Good morning, sunshine!" Gail greeted me with a warm smile. "I've made a special breakfast to celebrate your safe return and Sophia's as well."

I slid into my seat, my eyes widening in amazement at the feast before me. *Roy would be furious. Pancakes drenched in extra butter and syrup were the only way he would have eaten them, just like his mama used to make.*

Gail noticed my expression and asked, "What's wrong, honey?"

"I've never had pancakes with strawberries and whipped cream before."

"Well, you're in for a treat," Gail replied, placing a stack of pancakes on my plate and topping them with a generous helping of strawberries and whipped cream. "Dig in!"

I took a bite, and my taste buds exploded with the sweet and tangy flavors. "This is delicious!" I exclaimed, my mouth full.

Gail laughed. "I'm glad you like it. We deserve a little celebration after everything that's happened. The only thing left is to find Roy."

As if on cue, the phone rang. Gail wiped her hands on a towel and picked up the receiver. Her expression grew serious as she listened, then she nodded. "We'll be there," she said before hanging up.

"That was the sheriff," she informed me. "He wants you to come by the office after school for a few more questions."

I nodded, feeling a mix of curiosity and apprehension. "Do you think they're getting close to finding Roy?"

"I hope so," Gail said, a determined look in her eyes. "In the meantime, I'm going to talk to Judge Hopper today to see what needs to be done to get legal custody of you."

I looked up at her, my heart swelling with gratitude. "You really want to take custody of me?"

"Of course I do," Gail said, her voice gentle. "You're a part of my family now."

For the first time in what felt like forever, a sense of belonging washed over me. It seemed like all my troubles were finally starting to fade away. I reached for the wishing stone hanging from my necklace and held it in my hand, feeling its warmth seep into my skin. "I think my mama would have loved that idea."

Gail smiled, her eyes misting over. "I know she would have. She's watching over you, you know."

After breakfast, Gail drove me to school. As soon as we pulled up, kids started running toward us, their footsteps pounding against the pavement as they closed in. They surrounded me in an instant, their faces lit up with excitement and relief.

"I'm so glad you're okay!" one of them shouted, wrapping me in a tight hug that made it hard to breathe.

Before I could even catch my breath, Jill and Tricia pushed their way through the crowd and nearly tackled me with their hugs. They clung to me so tightly that I could barely move.

"We were so worried about you!" Jill cried, tears streaming down her cheeks.

Tricia nodded vigorously, her expression full of guilt and determination. "We should have done something about that clown. We should have paid more attention."

I shook my head, fighting back tears of my own. "It's not your fault," I said, my emotions swirling inside me. "You couldn't have known."

Just then, Mrs. Staggs, our teacher, approached with a beaming smile. "It's a wonderful day. I'm so happy you're safe," she said, patting my back gently. Her eyes sparkled with genuine joy as she looked at the scene unfolding around us. "Okay, everyone, let's head inside."

The kids reluctantly released me, their chatter full of excitement as they started toward the school building. I watched them go, feeling a mix of gratitude and a lingering unease. The nightmare wasn't over yet—Roy was still out there—but in that moment, I felt surrounded by love and support.

All day, everyone kept coming up to me, wrapping me in hugs and telling me how glad they were that I was okay. It was like the whole school had turned into one big celebration, with laughter and smiles everywhere I looked. For a moment, it almost felt like things were back to normal. But no matter how hard I tried to focus on the warmth and relief around me, Roy's shadow lingered in the back of my mind, darkening the edges of the joy.

After school, Gail picked me up, and we drove straight to the sheriff's office. The air was thick with tension as we walked in, and the sheriff greeted us with a serious expression before leading us to a small, dimly lit room.

"Loretta, Gail," he said, gesturing to the two chairs opposite him. "Please, have a seat."

Gail didn't waste a second. "Did you find anything about Roy?" she asked, her voice tight with anxiety.

The sheriff shook his head. "No, not yet. But we did find his wallet, not far from where Sophia was held."

My heart dropped, and I glanced at Gail, my eyes wide with fear. *Why was Roy's wallet there if it wasn't him?*

The sheriff turned his attention to me. "Loretta, do you know who the clown was that grabbed you?"

I swallowed hard, feeling my hands tremble in my lap. "I thought it was Roy," I whispered, my voice shaky.

He nodded, then pressed gently, "And the voice? Do you remember anything about it?"

I squeezed my eyes shut, trying to force the memory back, but all I could feel was the cold grip of fear from that night. "I... I can't remember," I admitted, frustration rising in my throat. *Why couldn't I just recall the details? Everything was a blur.*

The sheriff sighed, a deep crease forming between his brows. "Gary didn't write the 'TICK TOCK' note. It wasn't his handwriting. And we don't think the clown was Gary either."

"So, it was Roy," Gail interjected, leaning forward in her chair.

The sheriff held up a hand. "We don't know for sure. Firecracker claims that whoever grabbed her that night wasn't Roy. And we interviewed Sophia this morning; she said the person was heavy and shorter than Roy."

"What?" Gail's voice was tinged with both surprise and confusion. "But if it wasn't Roy, how did his wallet end up on the ground where Sophia was held?"

The sheriff leaned back in his chair, his expression grim. "That's what we're trying to figure out. The wallet could've been planted to throw us off, or Roy might still be involved somehow. We're considering every possibility."

"Oh, bull," Gail fumed, her voice rising with anger. "He's no good. He murdered Loretta's mom, abused Loretta, and God knows what else her poor mom went through."

The sheriff remained calm, but I could see the tension in his eyes. "Gail," he said, trying to keep his voice steady, "I know he deserves to be in prison…"

"In prison?" she shrieked, her eyes blazing. "That man deserves to rot in hell!"

The sheriff took a deep breath, clearly trying to stay composed. "We'll find out if he has anything to do with this. We're following every lead."

"Of course he does," she snapped, her voice dripping with conviction. "Who else would send Loretta and me that note? For God's sake, she's only ten years old! It's not likely she has any sick, demented enemies like that!"

"Calm down, Gail," the sheriff urged, his tone firm but measured.

That was the first time I'd ever seen Gail truly lose her cool. With her fiery red hair and a spirit as fierce as the nearby swamps, she was a force to be reckoned with when she was mad. But underneath all that fire, I could see the love and protectiveness driving her rage.

I reached out and took her hand. Our eyes met, and she managed a small smile despite her anger. It felt really good to know that someone cared that much about me—that she was ready to go to war if it meant keeping me safe.

More questions followed, each one making my heart race a little faster. By the time it was over, I felt like I could hardly breathe. As we stepped outside, Gail wrapped her arm around my shoulders, pulling me close. "You did really well in there," she murmured. "I know it wasn't easy, but we're going to get through this together."

I nodded, forcing a small smile, but my thoughts were still tangled in knots.

As we walked, Gail's expression softened. "Oh, and I almost forgot—I spoke with Judge Hopper this morning. He was very understanding. There's going to be some paperwork and a couple of court hearings, but he thinks we can make it work."

A wave of relief swept over me. "Seriously? That's amazing!" I could feel some of the tension in my chest finally easing.

Gail nodded, her smile warm but tired. "It's not going to be quick or easy, but he's on our side. We just need to stay patient and stick together." She gave my shoulder a reassuring squeeze. "You've been so strong through all of this. It's okay to feel scared or unsure, but remember—you're not alone."

Her words sunk in, and something inside me began to shift. Maybe things really could get better. "Thanks, Gail. I don't know what I'd do without you."

She stopped walking and turned to face me. "You're family. We're in this together, no matter what. We'll take it one step at a time."

I swallowed the lump in my throat and nodded, feeling the weight of everything, but also the comfort of knowing someone had my back.

"I also swung by Pelican Bay while you were at school and picked up a gift for Micky," Gail said as we drove. "If it weren't for him, who knows what might've happened? I'm so grateful he chose to open his shop here in Bayou Vista. We'll stop by and drop it off."

When we reached Micky's store, Gail handed me a beautifully wrapped box with a small card tucked under the ribbon. "Here, you can give it to him," she said, her voice soft but full of warmth.

I took the box, glancing at the card. The neat handwriting read, "Thank you, to my hero." My chest tightened as I carefully opened the box. Inside was a custom coffee cup with "My Hero" painted in elegant script, along with Micky's name on the side. Nestled beneath it were four large bags of specialty coffee. I couldn't help but smile at how perfect it was—simple, thoughtful, and exactly what Micky would love.

We walked into the store, and Micky greeted us with his usual warm smile. "Well, hello there! What brings you two by today?"

I took a deep breath and handed him the box, my hands trembling just a bit. "This is for you. Thank you for everything you've done for me."

Micky's eyes widened with surprise as he carefully untied the ribbon and lifted the lid. His face lit up. "You know me well—I can't function without my coffee!" he chuckled. "This is perfect. Thank you so much."

He pulled me into a hug, and I felt the genuine warmth of his gratitude wrap around me. But even as I hugged him back, a small part of me knew that no gift could ever truly repay him for what he'd given me. He didn't just save my life—he gave me a way to stay connected with my mama in a way I never thought possible.

Micky stepped back, his eyes soft with kindness. "Loretta," he said gently, "you didn't have to get me anything. Just knowing you're safe and happy—that's more than enough for me."

His words made my chest tighten with emotion, and I realized how much he truly cared. Micky wasn't just a hero to me; he was like family. And in this small moment, I knew how lucky I was to have him in my life.

Later that evening, Gail suggested we wind down with a movie. She popped some popcorn, and we curled up on the couch under a cozy blanket. "It's nice, isn't it?" she said, glancing over at me. "A quiet night in, just us."

I nodded, savoring the buttery popcorn and the simple joy of doing something normal. The movie was lighthearted, a welcome distraction from everything that had been weighing me down. For a while, I let myself get lost in it, laughing along with Gail at the silly parts. It felt good to just be a kid for once, without the shadow of fear hanging over me.

When the movie ended, we sat in comfortable silence for a moment. Gail looked over at me with a gentle smile.

"I'm so proud of how far you've come, Loretta. You deserve these peaceful moments."

I smiled back, feeling a warmth in my chest. "I just wish it could stay like this," I whispered. "If we could just catch Roy, maybe this nightmare would finally be over."

Gail's expression grew serious, but she squeezed my hand reassuringly. "We will, sweetie. He can't hide forever. And until then, you've got so many people who care about you. We'll keep you safe."

That night, I sat on my bed with Mr. Teddy in my lap, absentmindedly running my fingers over his worn button eyes. The familiar feel of the soft, frayed fabric brought a bittersweet comfort. But as I stared into those faded eyes, memories crept in—memories of Mom, of the night she was taken from me. The warmth of her voice, the way she held me close, it all felt so distant now, like a dream I could barely hold onto.

But no matter how hard I tried to stay in that memory, Roy's harsh voice always cut through, dragging me back to the reality I couldn't escape. The comfort I sought was shattered by the reminder that monsters weren't just made-up things lurking in the dark. They were real, and they lived right in my house, in the form of the man who was supposed to protect me.

I hugged Mr. Teddy tighter, the worn fur comforting in a way that almost felt like a hug from Mom. My chest ached with questions that never seemed to stop swirling in my mind. Was Gary really my dad? If he was, why didn't he protect me from Roy? And what if Roy found out Gary was trying to help me? Did he... did he kill him? Leave him out by the swamp for the alligators, just like the rumors said he did?

The thought sent a chill down my spine, cold and deep. I squeezed Mr. Teddy even harder, trying to push away the gnawing fear. But the questions stuck, twisting in my mind, refusing to let go.

Then, I thought about Gail. With her, there was a warmth I wasn't used to—a feeling of safety that almost felt foreign. She didn't look at me like I was a burden or someone she had to take care of out of obligation. With her, I felt like I mattered, like I was someone worth caring about. That warmth started to melt some of the cold fear inside me, making it easier to believe that maybe, just maybe, things could be different.

I wanted so badly to believe that things could get better, that with Gail's help, I might be able to leave the pain behind. But Roy's shadow was always there, lurking in the back of my mind, reminding me that the past isn't something you can just walk away from. He was still out there, and as long as he was, I couldn't fully escape the fear that clung to me, no matter how hard I tried to push it away.

~ 32 ~

WHISPERS AND RUMORS

The days that followed were a strange blend of ordinary and terrifying. School continued as if everything was normal, but the fear of Roy still being out there clung to us like a shadow. Every day brought new whispers—half-truths and wild guesses—but no real answers. It felt like the entire town was holding its breath.

One Saturday afternoon, I found myself at the library with Jill and Tricia. We huddled in a quiet corner, our voices low as we discussed the latest rumors.

"Do you think they'll ever catch him?" Jill asked, her voice barely above a whisper. Her wide eyes were filled with a worry that matched the tension I'd been feeling.

"I don't know," I replied, a heaviness settling in my chest. "It feels like he's always one step ahead, like he knows what's coming."

Tricia nodded slowly, her expression serious. "It's creepy, like he's somehow watching everything. How does he keep slipping away?"

For a moment, we sat in silence, the weight of the situation pressing down on us. The library, usually a place of comfort with its warm light and rows of books, suddenly felt different—cold, almost sinister. Even the sound of a turning page seemed too loud, as if any noise could draw unwanted attention.

Rosie Fontenot was sitting at the next table, as usual, buried in a stack of books with her scribbled notes spread out around her. When she caught me glancing her way, she narrowed her eyes and quickly stood up, gathering her things with an exaggerated huff.

As she passed by, she leaned in just enough for me to catch her sneer. "I guess they still haven't found your stepdaddy, huh?" she muttered, her voice laced with sarcasm before she let out a dark chuckle.

Jill's frown deepened. "What's her problem?"

I just rolled my eyes and shrugged it off. "She's always like that."

Comments about Roy had become a regular part of my life lately—people either pitied me or blamed me, and I was getting used to it. Everyone in town hated him, and by extension, some of that hate seemed to spill onto me.

But even as I tried to brush it off, Rosie's words stuck with me. No matter how much I wanted to forget, Roy's shadow followed me everywhere, even in the library, where I used to feel safe.

Later that day, as I walked home from Jill's house, an uneasy feeling settled over me. It started as a prickling at the back of my neck, then turned into a creeping dread that made my skin crawl. I quickened my pace, my heart pounding as I glanced over my shoulder every few steps. The street was empty, but that only made it worse—like someone could be hiding just out of sight. By the time I reached the house, I was breathless, my chest tight with panic.

Gail was sitting on the porch, her face softening with a smile that quickly vanished when she saw me. She rushed toward me, concern flashing in her eyes. "What happened? You look like you've seen a ghost."

I swallowed hard, trying to steady my voice. "I don't know... I just felt like someone was following me."

Gail's expression darkened with worry. "Why didn't someone walk home with you? You know you shouldn't be out alone until Roy's caught."

"I told them I'd be fine," I admitted, though my voice wavered, still shaky from the fear that clung to me.

Gail sighed, her expression softened. "We can't take any chances, not with everything going on. No more walking alone, okay? I'll talk to the sheriff and see if we can get more patrols in the area."

I nodded, but the uneasy feeling didn't fully go away. I couldn't shake the sense that Roy's shadow was still out there, lurking in the corners of my life. Until he was found, that fear would always be just a step behind me.

One evening, as Gail and I were chopping vegetables for dinner, a sharp knock echoed through the house. Gail's eyes met mine, a flicker of worry crossing her face before she wiped her hands on a towel and went to answer the door. The moment she opened it, I knew something was wrong. The sheriff stood there, his expression grim, the lines on his face more profound than usual.

"We've found something," he said, his voice low and heavy. "You both need to come with me."

My pulse quickened, a tight knot of fear forming in my stomach as we followed him out to his car. The ride was tense and suffocating, the silence amplifying the dread that hung in the air. I stared out the window at the familiar streets and shops as we drove toward the church at the edge of town.

As we neared Preacher's Pond—a place everyone in town avoided after dark—the mood shifted, thickening with an unsettling tension. The old rumors about a serial killer hunting his first victims here suddenly felt disturbingly real. The pond, with its murky waters and tangled reeds, had always been shrouded in whispers, but now it seemed like the perfect hiding place for something sinister, something waiting to be uncovered.

When we arrived, my breath caught in my throat. A line of patrol cars and officers stretched out near the edge of the woods by the old walking path, their faces grim and focused. Flashlights sliced through the deepening twilight, revealing a small clearing where a crowd had gathered. The sheriff motioned for us to follow, his footsteps crunching over brittle leaves as we moved deeper into the clearing. The closer we got, the colder the air grew, thick with a heavy sense of dread, as if the forest itself held its breath.

Then I saw it—a shallow grave, freshly uncovered in the dirt. My stomach twisted as we approached, the officers standing in a tight circle, their faces drawn with the horror of what they had uncovered. One of them stepped aside, revealing what lay inside.

I had to fight the urge to look away. The sight in front of me was more than just horrifying—it was a brutal reminder of how close evil had come, how it had wormed its way into our lives like a slow-acting poison. The remains were barely recognizable, twisted and decayed, yet they told a story—a story of pain and suffering, of someone who had met a fate I could hardly bear to imagine.

"Don't look," the sheriff said quietly, stepping in front of me to block the view, but it was too late. The image was already burned into my mind.

"Oh my God," Gail gasped, gripping my hand so tightly it hurt. "Who... who is that?" Her voice was shaky, but her eyes stayed glued to the scene, unable to look away.

The sheriff's voice was low and thick with emotion. "We're not sure yet... but we think this could be tied to Roy."

A cold shiver ran down my spine, sharper than the chill in the air. Just when I thought we might find some peace, our world was about to be turned upside down again. I felt a wave of nausea roll through me, and Gail immediately wrapped her arm around my shoulders, her voice soft in my ear. "It's okay, honey. Just breathe."

The sheriff crouched down, holding up something that caught the light—a pair of red mirrored sunglasses with a copper frame. "Do these look familiar?"

My heart dropped. "Y-yes," I stammered, my voice barely a whisper. "They're Roy's."

His expression grew even more serious. "Did Roy ever bring you out here?"

I nodded, the memories flooding back in sharp flashes. "H-he used to take me fishing here."

The sheriff exchanged a look with one of the officers before pulling another object from a plastic bag. "We also found this inside the grave," he said, holding up an oval gold locket with the letter 'C' engraved on it. He carefully opened it, revealing a faded photo of me as a little girl, smiling next to my mom. "It looks like Roy held onto Caroline's locket all these years."

Tears welled up in my eyes, spilling over as I stared at the locket. It was like the past had come crashing back, all the pain and fear that I'd tried so hard to bury. My chest tightened, and I couldn't hold it in any longer—I broke down, sobs shaking my whole body.

Gail pulled me close, rubbing my back as she said softly, "I think you've seen enough. Let's get you home."

The sheriff nodded, his expression heavy. "I'm sorry you had to see this."

As we walked away, I could still feel the weight of the locket, the lingering fear, and the inescapable truth that as long as Roy was out there, nothing would ever truly be safe.

On the drive home, a wave of nausea churned in my stomach. The horrifying truth gnawed at me—I'd been living with a monster my entire life, and I never even knew it. The image of the grave and that locket wouldn't leave my mind.

The next day at school, the tension was almost suffocating. Word about what was found had spread like wildfire, and the whole town was buzzing with fear and speculation. Classes carried on, but everyone was distracted, their eyes darting nervously toward me when they thought I wasn't looking. Whispers followed me down the hall, like they were all waiting for something more to unravel. I could feel the tension whenever I passed by, the unspoken questions hanging in the air—what was it like living with a monster, and how much did I really know?

At lunch, Jill, Tricia, and I sat together, but our usual chatter was replaced with uneasy silence. We picked at our food, the mood heavy with unspoken fears.

"Do you think they'll figure out who it is?" Tricia finally asked, her voice barely above a whisper, as if saying it any louder would make it more real.

"I don't know," I said, my thoughts racing. "But they have to. Maybe this time, the sheriff will get some answers."

Jill glanced around, her face pale. "It's terrifying that Roy is still out there. What if he's hiding close by, watching? What if he's planning something?"

We fell silent again, each of us trapped in our own anxious thoughts. The cafeteria, usually loud and buzzing with noise, felt eerily quiet. My mind kept drifting back to that locket. Why had Roy kept it? Was it some kind of sick trophy? It couldn't have been out of love—Roy didn't know the first thing about love. Everything he did was twisted by hatred and cruelty.

The more I thought about it, the sicker I felt. That locket wasn't just a piece of jewelry—it was a symbol of everything Roy had taken from me.

The rest of the day passed in a fog, the lessons just background noise to the anxiety buzzing in my head. When the final bell rang, I grabbed my things and rushed out, relieved to escape.

Gail was waiting for me outside, leaning against the car with a worried look on her face. "How was your day?" she asked gently as I approached.

I shrugged, staring down at the gravel. "It was... fine, I guess," I said, but my voice sounded hollow. "Everyone's freaked out, talking about Roy."

Gail sighed, her eyes soft with concern. "I know it's hard, but we're going to get through this. We just have to take it one day at a time, okay?"

I nodded, but the reassurance didn't sink in. Everything still felt heavy, like a dark cloud hanging over us that wouldn't go away.

That evening, as we sat quietly in the living room, the phone rang, cutting through the tense silence. Gail picked it up, her face tight with worry. But as she listened, her expression softened with a mix of relief and concern. "Thank you for letting us know, Sheriff. We appreciate the update."

After she hung up, she turned to me with a hopeful tone. "They've identified the remains. It was one of the missing women—Mary Campbell. The sheriff thinks this might be the break they've been waiting for."

A wave of nausea hit me as a memory suddenly flashed through my mind—the dirty shovel and bloody clothes I'd seen in the back of Roy's pickup. My stomach twisted as I struggled to find the words. "Gail... that shovel and those clothes I saw in Roy's truck... what if—"

Gail's eyes widened in realization, her hand flying to her mouth. "Oh my God," she whispered, her voice trembling. "I need to call the sheriff."

She grabbed the phone, her fingers shaking as she dialed. I could feel the weight of what this meant pressing down on both of us—it was suffocating. This wasn't just some distant horror story; it was real, and it was happening in our lives.

When she hung up, her composure cracked. Tears welled up in her eyes, and she covered her face with her hands as she began to cry. "Mary's mom was at the sheriff's office when I called," she choked out. "That poor woman... I can't even imagine what she's going through."

Seeing Gail break down like that made everything feel even more real. The truth was no longer something we could keep at a distance. It was here, closing in on us, and it was more horrifying than I could have ever imagined.

~ 33 ~

WHO'S THERE?

I lay in bed that night, clutching Mr. Teddy tightly against my chest. The soft rustling of leaves outside drifted in through the cracked window, making shadows flicker across the walls like something was moving out there. I gripped the wishing stone, its cool weight in my hand usually grounding me, but tonight it wasn't enough. Every creak and groan of the old house made me tense up, my mind racing with fears I couldn't quite push away.

Suddenly, a faint whisper cut through the stillness—so soft I almost convinced myself I imagined it. My heart pounded as I sat up, straining to listen, every nerve on edge.

"Who's there?" I whispered, my voice barely more than a shaky breath. But there was no reply—only an unnerving silence that made every creak and rustle in the house feel sharper, more sinister.

I clutched the wishing stone tighter, its smooth surface warming in my palm. I closed my eyes and focused on the thought of my mama, trying to draw comfort from her memory. But instead of calming me, the shadows seemed to crowd closer, thickening around me like they were alive, pressing in from every corner of the room.

A sudden, loud thump from the front porch made me jump, my heart slamming against my chest. I held my breath, straining to hear, trying to convince myself it was just the old house settling. But it didn't feel like that—it felt different, more deliberate.

My pulse raced as I slipped out of bed, tiptoeing to the door and slowly cracking it open. The hallway stretched out in front of me, bathed in a faint, eerie glow from the moonlight filtering through the windows. The light only made the shadows seem darker, twisting into shapes that played tricks on my mind.

I took a deep breath and forced myself to step into the hallway. The floorboards groaned beneath me, each creak sending a fresh wave of unease crawling up my spine. With every cautious step, the quiet seemed to grow heavier, pressing in on me. I couldn't shake the unsettling sense that something—or someone—was watching from the shadows. Every little noise—an old pipe creaking, the rustle of leaves outside—felt unnaturally loud, making the short walk to the front of the house feel like it stretched on forever.

The warmth of the wishing stone pulsed faintly in my hand, a small comfort that barely held back the rising panic. When I finally reached the living room, I froze, listening hard for any sound that might give away what I was so afraid of. The silence hung thick in the air, but a prickling sensation ran down the back of my neck. It was that unmistakable feeling—you just know you're not alone, even if you can't see it.

I swallowed hard, my ears straining for any hint of movement, every second dragging out the tension. The shadows seemed darker, deeper, like they were hiding something just out of sight.

In the dim light, I noticed the front door slightly ajar, swaying gently in the breeze. My breath hitched, a chill running through me. Someone had been inside.

Forcing myself to stay calm, I crept toward the door, every instinct screaming at me to run the other way. I closed it carefully, the soft click of the lock echoing through the quiet house. But as I turned back, something flickered in the mirror down the hallway—a shadow, quick and fleeting, darting across the room.

My heart pounded as I whipped around, but the room was empty. I took a shaky step back, clutching the stone so tightly my knuckles ached. A cold breeze brushed past my cheek, and then I heard it again—the whisper, clearer this time: *"TICK TOCK, Loretta."*

The words sent a jolt of terror through me. "It's Roy," I muttered, barely recognizing my own voice. Panic clawed at me, but I swallowed it down, refusing to let it take control. I gripped the stone and whispered, "Mama, please help me."

To my surprise, the stone grew warmer, a gentle heat radiating through my hand. A sense of calm slowly spread over me, dulling the sharp edges of fear. I took a deep breath, and the darkness seemed to pull back just a little.

But then—a faint knock came from the back door. My body tensed, every muscle screaming for me to freeze, but I couldn't. I spun around, heart hammering in my chest, eyes locked on the direction of the sound. I didn't know what I'd find, but I knew I couldn't just stand there.

Summoning every ounce of courage, I started toward the back of the house, my steps shaky but determined. The whispers of fear still echoed in my mind, but I refused to let them take over. Whatever was waiting for me, I had to face it.

I hesitated as I reached the door, my hand hovering over the handle. My heart thudded in my chest, and I could feel the trembling in my fingers. Taking a shaky breath, I finally mustered the courage and flung the door open, bracing myself for whatever might be out there.

But there was nothing—just the empty darkness of the night, the wind rustling through the trees, and the faint creak of branches swaying. The cold air brushed against my skin, doing little to ease the tension in my chest.

I stood there for a moment, scanning the shadows, half-expecting something to lunge out at me. But the yard was still, the only movement coming from the swaying leaves. My breath slowly steadied, though the unease gnawed at me.

Finally, I closed the door and locked it, making sure it was secure. Leaning back against it, I let out a long breath, a mix of relief and lingering fear twisting in my gut. Even with the door locked, the sense of dread hadn't fully left—it clung to the edges of my mind, reminding me that this wasn't over, not by a long shot.

"Loretta?" Gail's voice whispered from the hallway, tinged with concern. "Is that you?"

"Yeah," I replied softly, barely finding my voice.

She hurried over to me, her eyes scanning my face. "What are you doing up? Are you okay?"

"The front door was open," I stammered, my voice trembling. "I thought I heard someone."

Gail's brows knitted in confusion as she rushed to the door, checking the lock and peering outside. "That's impossible. I locked it myself before bed." She turned back to me, her face tight with worry.

Tears welled up in my eyes. "It was Roy! He whispered, 'TICK TOCK, Loretta.' He's here, Gail! He's here!"

Gail's face went pale, but she didn't hesitate. She flicked on every light in the house, her movements quick and deliberate as she checked every room—closets, under beds, corners, windows, even behind the curtains. I stood frozen in place, watching her, trying to convince myself it was just my imagination.

After what felt like an eternity, she came back, her expression softer but still tense. "There's no one here, sweetie," she said, gently pulling me into a hug. "I think it's the stress of everything—the call from the sheriff, everything you've been through. Roy would have to be crazy to come anywhere near you now."

But her words didn't fully sink in. I could feel her trying to be strong for me, but the tremor in her voice told me she was scared too.

"Would you feel better if we slept in the living room tonight?" she asked, her tone reassuring.

I nodded, even though I hated admitting it. "Yeah," I whispered, my voice shaky. I didn't want to worry her more, but the truth was, I didn't want to be alone.

"Okay," she said, grabbing some blankets and pillows. "I'm staying close. You take the recliner, and I'll be right here on the loveseat, just in case."

I climbed into the recliner and pulled the covers up to my chin, trying to find comfort in Gail's presence. But even with the lights on and her nearby, I couldn't shake the feeling that someone—or something—was still watching, waiting just out of sight in the shadows.

~ 34 ~

THE RECKONING!

Two years drifted by like a foggy memory, the kind that lingers just out of reach but leaves a sense of unease. Every lead on Roy evaporated into nothing, one dead end after another. Yet, his presence still lingered over Bayou Vista like a ghost. Each time the phone rang, my heart would leap with hope, only to sink again when it wasn't the news I was desperate to hear—just more disappointment, more unanswered questions.

The town tried to move forward, but fear had a way of clinging to everything. It was in the way people spoke in hushed tones, the extra locks on doors, the wary glances over shoulders. Women kept disappearing—not just from Bayou Vista, but from Pelican Bay and Cypress Cove too. It felt endless, each case a grim reminder that the threat wasn't just lingering—it was growing bolder.

The patterns that once seemed deliberate, almost calculated, had unraveled into something far more chaotic and terrifying. No one knew where or when it would strike next. It was like living under a constant shadow, always bracing for the next terrible thing to happen.

Jason's Bar used to be the place everyone feared—the spot people whispered about when the disappearances first began. But that had changed. The unsettling truth was that the kidnappings were no longer confined to one place or even one type of venue. The pattern was gone, replaced by random chaos. Women were being taken from grocery store parking lots, gas stations, even their own front yards. It didn't matter where you were or how cautious you tried to be—nowhere felt safe anymore.

The fear had spread like a slow poison through the town. The small comfort people once felt in knowing which places to avoid had been shattered. Now, every ordinary outing carried the weight of uncertainty. No one knew when the next person would vanish, only that it was inevitable.

Gary turned out to be my biological father. Even now, no one fully understands why he kept it a secret or why he stayed silent while I suffered under Roy's abuse. It's like he was watching from the sidelines, knowing the truth but choosing to do nothing. That made it all the harder to accept—he could've done something, but he didn't.

In true small-town fashion, the rumors spiraled out of control. People whispered that Gary and my mom had been having an affair right up until the time Roy killed her. Some folks were convinced that Roy found out and murdered her in a jealous rage. But separating fact from gossip in a place like Bayou Vista is nearly impossible. Everyone had their own version of events, but when it came down to it, no one really knew the truth. The lines between what actually happened and what people wanted to believe had blurred beyond recognition.

After everything that happened, Gail got custody of me. It was a big change, but one that brought a glimmer of hope in the middle of all the chaos. We packed up our things and left behind the old neighborhood, the place where every corner seemed to hold a painful memory of Roy. Leaving that house felt like finally letting go of a weight I'd been carrying for too long. With each mile that took us further away, it felt like some of the darkness we'd been living under started to fade.

We moved into a small house on the beach, just a couple of blocks from town. The new place was modest but cozy, with warm colors and a front porch where we could sit and watch the waves roll in. It wasn't fancy, but it felt like a fresh start. Mornings meant stepping outside with our toes in the sand, the salty breeze ruffling our hair as the sun crept over the horizon. The house had everything we needed—bright rooms filled with sunlight, windows that let in the sound of the gulls, and, most importantly, a sense of safety that had been missing for so long.

For the first time in my life, I started to believe that maybe, just maybe, we could find some peace here. The past still lingered, but it felt a little more distant now, like it was finally something I could leave behind.

To help make our new house feel even more like home, Gail adopted a puppy. Coco, a delightful little poodle-terrier mix with a fluffy coat and bright, curious eyes, quickly became a bundle of joy in our lives. I was the one who named her Coco, inspired by her sweet, cocoa-colored fur. The puppy's playful antics and boundless energy brought a sense of normalcy and happiness that we had both missed for so long.

Coco quickly settled into our new routine, her wagging tail and playful bark filling the house with laughter and light. She was a constant companion, always there to cheer me up and remind me that, despite everything, there was still room for joy.

One cold morning, as the fog clung to the bayou like a shroud, the phone rang. This time, I could tell by the way Gail tensed that it wasn't another false alarm.

She answered, her face paling as she listened. "Yes, Sheriff, we'll be there as soon as we can."

When she hung up, she turned to me, her eyes wide with a mixture of shock and something else—relief, maybe, but it was hard to tell.

"They found Roy," she said quietly. "His body."

My heart pounded in my chest. "Where?"

"At the old campground," she replied, almost in disbelief. "Tied to a tree."

I stared at her, struggling to process the words. The man who had haunted my every nightmare was gone—dead. But instead of the overwhelming relief I expected, all I felt was a dull numbness, like my brain couldn't catch up with what my heart was feeling.

"The sheriff wants us there," Gail continued, "but you don't have to go if you're not ready."

"No," I said firmly, surprising myself with the conviction in my voice. "I need to see it with my own eyes, to know this nightmare is really over."

We drove in silence, the gravel crunching under the tires as we made our way toward the campground. The place had once been filled with the sounds of laughter, kids roasting marshmallows, families telling ghost stories around the fire. Now, it was the site of a real-life horror—where Roy murdered my mom. There was something grimly ironic about it—his life ending in the same place where his darkness first touched mine.

As we got closer, a knot tightened in my stomach. Seeing the sheriff's lights flickering through the trees made it all feel terrifyingly real. I wasn't sure what I'd feel when I saw Roy's body, but I knew I had to face it—to put this chapter to rest, no matter how twisted the ending was.

The sheriff met us at the entrance, his expression grave. "It's not easy to see," he said, his voice low, "but I think you need to."

We followed him down the overgrown path, the trees looming overhead, their twisted branches like dark fingers reaching out. The air was heavy with the damp smell of earth and something else—something sour and decaying. As we neared the clearing, the flashing blue and red lights flickered through the trees, casting eerie shadows. The murmurs of officers and the crunch of footsteps on dead leaves made everything feel surreal, like a nightmare I couldn't wake from.

And then I saw him. Roy's body was tied to an old oak tree, his head slumped forward, eyes staring blankly at nothing. A shiver ran through me, ice cold and deep. He was right there—right by the spot where he had buried my mom all those years ago. The scene was brutal. His wrists were bound tightly with rope, his mouth gagged with a dirty cloth. But what really made my stomach twist was the message carved into his chest: "Justice Served."

Gail let out a choked gasp and instinctively covered her mouth, her eyes wide with horror. "Who could have done this?" she whispered, her voice trembling.

The sheriff's face was tense as he shook his head. "We're still figuring that out. It looks like the work of a vigilante. Maybe someone connected to one of the missing women."

I couldn't tear my eyes away from the sight—fear, disbelief, and a mix of other emotions all churning inside me. I thought I'd feel nothing but relief now that the monster was dead, but instead, there was a strange emptiness. This wasn't how I imagined it ending—not like this.

I stepped closer, my heart pounding as I read the words carved into Roy's skin: "Justice Served." A flicker of happiness stirred in me, even through the unease. Roy was finally gone, and with him, the constant fear that had loomed over my life like a shadow. Relief washed over me, but it was tangled with everything else—like a knot too tight to fully untangle. I'd imagined what it would be like to see him gone for good, but standing here, the reality felt messier than I expected.

As I stared at his lifeless body, a sense of closure finally settled in. The monster was gone, and the nightmare that had haunted me was over. This chapter in my life is finished. The scars will remain, but for the first time, I can see a future beyond the fear—a chance to finally move forward.

The sheriff turned to us, his expression serious. "We need to keep this quiet for now. The last thing we need is a panic."

Gail nodded, but I could see the questions in her eyes.

As we walked back to the car, an uneasy feeling gnawed at me, like eyes were on us from somewhere in the trees. The wind rustled the branches, almost like it was carrying whispers—secrets buried deep in this place. I kept glancing over my shoulder, half-expecting to see something move in the shadows. But there was nothing—just the empty woods.

That night, I lay in bed, staring at the ceiling, sleep nowhere in sight. The image of Roy's lifeless body kept flashing in my mind, vivid and unsettling. I thought I'd feel relieved, like a weight had finally been lifted. But instead, my thoughts spun in circles, replaying the scene over and over, struggling to grasp that the monster was finally dead.

~ 35 ~

ECHOS OF SILENCE

The morning sun bathed Bayou Vista in warm, golden light, almost as if the town itself was relieved that Roy was gone for good. Word of his grim fate spread quickly, fueling the usual gossip. In a town where everyone knows everyone's business, rumors were as common as morning coffee. Some folks whispered that a grieving father had finally snapped and taken justice into his own hands; others believed it was an outsider settling an old score. The stories grew more outlandish with each retelling, but no one really knew the truth.

The sheriff's investigation turned up nothing—no fingerprints, no witnesses, no leads. It was as if the vigilante had vanished without a trace, leaving behind only questions. And while the case slowly slipped into the background, the unease didn't completely fade.

Sheriff Johnson never uncovered the truth behind the clown who grabbed me that night. He dismissed it as

Roy's doing, like most of the town did, but whispers linger about a far older terror—a man who murdered his entire family fifty years ago while dressed as a clown. They say he vanished without a trace, leaving behind a legacy of fear. The old house still stands at the edge of town near Devil's Hollow Marsh, its windows like empty eyes staring out into the decaying reeds. No one stays there long. Those foolish enough to buy the house next door always seem to disappear. The townsfolk say the curse is tied to the marsh—a cursed ground where shadows move on their own. But it's the clown that haunts their nightmares—the one who was never caught, who may still be lurking, waiting for the next unlucky soul to cross his path.

In the weeks that followed, the town began a tentative journey toward healing. The constant tension eased, and life gradually returned to a fragile sense of normalcy. People started going about their daily routines again, but the memory of Roy's terror still lingered in quiet conversations and cautious glances.

His name was spoken in hushed tones, like saying it too loudly might somehow bring the darkness back. There was relief in knowing he was gone, a sense that the nightmare had finally ended. Reports of disappearances stopped, and the town began to breathe a little easier. With Roy no longer a threat, there was a cautious hope that Bayou Vista could finally move forward, even if the scars would always remain.

One evening, as the sun dipped below the horizon, Gail, Patricia, Margie, and I settled onto the porch with our glasses of sweet tea. The cool breeze brushed against us, offering a contrast to the tea's sugary warmth. We spent most evenings like this—watching the sunset, savoring the quiet moments. The steady rhythm of the ocean waves created a soothing backdrop to our conversation.

Gail stared out at the water, lost in thought. After a long silence, she sighed. "Do you think we'll ever know who did it?"

I took a sip of tea, mulling over the question. "Maybe. But maybe it's one of those things we're better off not knowing."

Patricia looked at me, concern creasing her brow. "You really think that?"

I hesitated, choosing my words carefully. "Whoever did it got rid of the monster that ruined my life. That counts for something, doesn't it?"

Gail nodded slowly. "It does."

Patricia still seemed uneasy. "But what if the vigilante isn't really a hero? What if they were just another killer?"

Margie frowned, shaking her head. "I've heard that too. Whoever it was, they're either really brave or dangerously reckless."

Gail looked thoughtful. "Micky kept saying he didn't think Roy was behind all those disappearances. Maybe someone framed him."

Margie shrugged. "Either way, Roy got what was coming to him."

Patricia let out a heavy sigh. "I just want the truth, but it's like we're all stuck in this never-ending uncertainty."

Gail turned to Patricia, her expression serious. "We're all searching for answers, but sometimes they take time."

Margie nodded in agreement. "The truth has a way of coming out eventually."

We let the conversation fade, carried away by the salty breeze and the sound of waves in the distance. The sky was awash in soft pinks and oranges, the last bit of sunlight glinting off the water. It was peaceful in a way that felt almost strange, like the calm after a storm when everything is still, but you know the ground is still settling beneath you.

That evening, as Gail and I took a slow walk through the streets of Bayou Vista, I noticed a subtle shift in the air. The fear that had gripped the town for so long had loosened its hold, replaced by a cautious hope. People were starting to breathe easier, like they were slowly waking up from a bad dream. Life was finding its rhythm again—more smiles, more laughter, even the simple joy of neighbors stopping to chat on their front porches. The town was healing, even if some wounds would never fully close.

Gail, Patricia, Margie, and I kept up our evening porch gatherings, sharing stories and talking about what the future might hold. The mystery of the vigilante lingered in the background, but it didn't dominate our thoughts the way it used to. People were more focused on moving forward, on rebuilding the sense of community that fear had chipped away at. The town wasn't quite the same, but in a way, it felt stronger—like it had been tested and found a way to survive.

For the first time in a long while, Bayou Vista felt like a place where hope was more than just a wish—it was something real, something that could finally take root and grow.

~ 36 ~

THE OLD ROUTINE

Jill, Tricia, and I decided it was time to return to our old routine. We made our way through town, feeling the warmth of the day and the familiar rhythm of Bayou Vista's bustling streets.

Our first stop was St. Theresa's Church. Preacher John met us at the door with his usual friendly smile.

"Morning, girls! How's it going?" he called out.

"We're good, Preacher John," Jill said. "Just making our rounds like always."

He chuckled. "That's what I like to hear. Y'all behave yourselves now!"

Next, we headed over to C&D Kwik Stop. Cindy was behind the counter, ringing up a customer, while Dondi was stacking shelves and gave us a quick nod.

"Hey there, girls!" Cindy greeted us with a smile. "What brings y'all in today?"

"We're just stopping by," Tricia said, taking a look around. "Trying to get back into our usual routine."

"That's good to hear!" Cindy said as she reached for a few sodas and handed them to us. "And Dondi's got a little something for you, too."

Dondi came over with a grin and handed each of us a candy bar. "On the house, ladies. Enjoy!"

"Thanks, Mr. Dondi!" we chimed together, grinning as we unwrapped the treats.

Our next stop was Shanster Travels, where Shannon was busy organizing travel brochures.

"Hey, Ms. Shannon!" I called out with a wave. "How's everything going?"

She looked up, her face brightening. "Hey, Loretta! Keeping busy as always, but can't complain. You girls planning any trips?"

"Not today," Jill said, shaking her head. "Just enjoying a stroll around town."

Shannon smiled and nodded. "That sounds like the perfect way to spend the day."

At Catrina's Closet, we found Catrina busy rearranging clothes on the racks. She looked up and greeted us with a warm smile.

"Hey, girls! Looking for anything in particular today?"

"Just browsing," Tricia said, eyeing the display. "Those new sweaters are really nice."

"Thanks!" Catrina said, clearly pleased. "Let me know if you need help with anything."

Next door, a new shop was getting ready to open. A lady with long blonde hair was standing on the sidewalk, taking notes in front of the large display window.

"Hi, girls," she said with a warm smile. "My name is Cindy Blevins."

"Hi," I said, returning her smile. "I'm Loretta. This is Jill," I pointed, "and that's Tricia."

"What kind of store are you opening?" Jill asked, curiosity evident in her voice.

"I'm thinking of selling candles, chocolates, lingerie—anything with a romantic vibe," Cindy said with a playful grin.

We all giggled at the list.

"What's the name of the store?" Tricia asked, curiosity piqued.

"Burning Love," Cindy replied with a wink. "You girls might not get the full meaning now, but trust me, you will when you're older."

We blushed and shook our heads. "I don't think so, Ms. Cindy," I said, half-laughing.

"Oh, you will," Cindy replied with a knowing smile. "But feel free to stop by anytime for a chat."

"Okay," we all said in unison, still giggling as we exchanged amused glances.

Our next stop was Frog's Delight Bakery, where LaDonna was chatting with a red-haired woman behind the counter.

"Hey, Ms. LaDonna!" I said, grinning.

"Hey, sweetie!" LaDonna replied, handing us each a warm cookie. "Girls, this is my sister Evelyn. She's just joined us, so be sure to make her feel welcome."

"Nice to meet you, Ms. Evelyn," Jill said with a friendly smile. "Are you learning the secret to making these delicious cookies?"

Evelyn laughed softly, her shyness fading a bit. "I'm trying, but I think that's a family secret LaDonna's holding onto for now."

LaDonna chuckled and winked. "She's got potential, though. Give her time."

At Bayou Bliss, Brenda was deep in conversation with Gail, Patricia, and Margie, all of them laughing and sipping coffee. She looked up and grinned as we walked in.

"Well, look who it is! Hello, darlings," Brenda said, her eyes sparkling. "You three are a sight for sore eyes."

"Hey, Ms. Brenda!" Tricia said. "How's business treating you?"

"Busy and blessed," Brenda replied with a warm smile. "These ladies here are buzzing about the new jewelry shop they're planning to open soon."

"That's exciting!" I said, smiling. "I can't wait to see it all come together."

As we walked past the offices, we spotted Judge Hopper and Mayor Strittmatter outside, talking by the steps. They both looked up and waved back with friendly smiles.

At Tanya's Crawfish Shack, Tanya was in her usual spot behind the counter, dishing out food with her usual energy.

"Hey, Ms. Tanya!" Jill called out. "It smells incredible in here, as always!"

"Thanks, girls!" Tanya said with a grin, handing us each a small sample. "I'm glad you stopped by. Don't be strangers!"

Our next stop was the library, where Lena, Terrie, and Amanda were busy sorting through stacks of books.

"Hey, everyone!" I called out. "How's everything going?"

"Pretty good," Lena said, looking up with a smile. "We're gearing up for a big event next week."

"That sounds fun!" Tricia said. "We'll definitely swing by and check it out."

As we walked past Jason's Bar, we spotted Jason outside, wiping down one of the tables.

"Hey, Mr. Jason!" I called out with a wave.

He looked up and grinned. "Hey, Loretta! How's it going?"

"Can't complain," I said. "Just out enjoying the town."

"Good to hear," Jason replied, leaning on the table. "It's a bit slow around here today, but I don't mind. Nice to see some friendly faces."

Our last stop was Berry's Market. Mike and Kathy were busy stocking shelves while Mrs. Staggs and Matilda browsed the aisles. Taylor and Laurrie were handling a line of customers at the checkout.

"Hey, Mr. Mike! Hey, Ms. Kathy!" we called out. "Looks like y'all are swamped!"

Mike flashed a grin. "Just keeping up with the rush. How're you girls doing?"

"We're good," I said, glancing over at Mrs. Staggs. "It's nice to see her out and about."

Mrs. Staggs looked up and waved. "Well, look at you girls! You're really growing up. I miss having you in my class."

"We miss you too," I replied with a smile.

While we were chatting, Firecracker came out from the back with a tray of mini cupcakes.

"Hey, y'all!" Firecracker said with a smile, holding out the tray. "Thought you might like a little treat."

"Thanks, Firecracker!" Jill said, eagerly grabbing a cupcake. "These look so good."

"Glad you think so!" Firecracker said with a playful wink.

Jill took a bite and grinned. "Mmm, it's delicious!"

Mike chuckled, grabbing a cupcake for himself. "You're not the only one who thinks so," he said before taking a big bite, his face lighting up with satisfaction.

We all laughed, enjoying the sweet moment together.

Finally, we headed to Micky's Magical Things. As soon as we walked in, Micky's face lit up with a big smile.

"Well, if it isn't my favorite girls! Loretta, Jill, Tricia—welcome!" Micky said, throwing his arms wide.

"Hi, Micky!" I said, grinning. "We couldn't end the day without stopping by."

Micky led us to the back of the store, where he'd set up a small display. "I've got something special for each of you," he said, pulling out three small boxes.

"What is it?" I asked, curiosity piqued.

Micky opened the boxes one by one, revealing beautiful charm bracelets, each with different handcrafted charms. "Just a little something to remind you all of your journey and how far you've come."

"Oh wow, Micky, these are perfect!" I said, holding mine up to admire it. Jill and Tricia were already slipping theirs on. "Thank you so much!"

"It's the least I could do," Micky said, his eyes warm with pride. "You girls have grown a lot, and I couldn't be prouder."

The sheriff walked in, giving us a friendly nod. "Hey, girls! Good to see y'all out and about again." He handed Micky a folder. "Take a look at this when you get a minute."

"Sure thing, Sheriff," Micky said, sliding the file behind the counter.

The sheriff tipped his hat. "Y'all have fun now," he said before heading out the door.

As soon as he left, I couldn't hold back my curiosity. "Is he still trying to track down the vigilante?"

"Yeah," Micky said with a serious look. "The vigilante... and the real killer."

Jill's eyes widened. "But Roy was the killer!"

Micky shook his head. "Roy was a monster, no doubt about that, and he got what was coming to him. But he wasn't the one behind all those murders."

"Then who is it?" Tricia asked, her voice low.

Micky's expression grew thoughtful. "I've got a feeling the vigilante and the killer might be one and the same."

Jill and Tricia exchanged uneasy glances.

"Don't start worrying," Micky said, trying to reassure us. "You girls are safe."

We let out a collective sigh of relief.

We spent the rest of the afternoon with Micky, enjoying the easy comfort of his company. By the time we left his store, I felt a deep sense of contentment. The shops in Bayou Vista weren't just places to buy things; they were the lifeblood of the town, each one reflecting the resilience and spirit of the people who lived here.

The day had been filled with familiar faces and warm conversations, reminding me just how much this town felt like home. With every stop we made, it was clear that, even with everything the town had been through, the connections we shared were stronger than ever.

As the sun began to set, washing the sky in shades of gold and orange, we made our way home. In that quiet moment, everything felt like it was falling back into place, like the world was right where it was supposed to be.

~ 37 ~

EPILOGUE

I stood at the edge of Bayou Vista, gazing out over the Gulf of Mexico as the sun began its gentle ascent. The waves lapped softly at the shore, and the first light of dawn bathed everything in a warm, golden hue. It was a scene I had witnessed countless times before, but today, it felt profoundly different. Today was the start of a new chapter in my life.

At nineteen, I was finally heading off to college—a dream Gail had helped make a reality. It was my chance to see what life had to offer beyond our small town, to figure out who I really was. I was excited for what lay ahead, but a part of me would always stay here, tied to the people and memories that made me who I am. Bayou Vista wasn't just a place—it was home, and no matter where life took me, that wouldn't change.

Tricia and Jill, my best friends through thick and thin, stood by my side, their smiles filled with pride and a touch of sadness.

Tricia, ever the adventurous spirit with dreams too grand for Bayou Vista, had flourished into a gifted writer. Her stories captivated readers far and wide, with her latest novel—drawn from the events that once haunted our town—achieving bestseller status. Now, she was already deep into her next project, fueled by the same passion and creativity that had brought her so much success.

Jill had married Anthony, her high school sweetheart, and together, they had crafted a beautiful life. Their grand house, perched on a sprawling estate at the edge of town, with its enchanting wraparound porch, looked like something from a fairy tale. They radiated pure happiness, and I couldn't have been more thrilled for them. Jill truly deserved every bit of joy, especially after all we had been through together.

"Promise you'll visit often," Tricia said, her voice catching slightly as she hugged me.

I nodded, hugging her back tightly. "I promise. And you better keep writing those amazing stories. Don't forget, I'm your biggest fan."

Jill's eyes glistened with tears as she embraced me next. "We're so proud of you, Loretta. Go out there and show the world what you're made of."

I smiled, blinking back my own tears. "Thank you. I wouldn't be here without you guys."

Micky, my mentor and friend, stood a little apart, watching us with a gentle smile. His shop, Micky's Magical Things, had always been a sanctuary for me—a place where I discovered the magic within myself. I spent every summer working with Micky, and over the years, he taught me more than I could ever repay him for.

He showed me that magic wasn't really about spells, potions, crystals, or oracle cards; it was about trusting in yourself and tapping into the power of your dreams. He taught me that we can shape our future if we truly believe in the vision we hold for ourselves. Micky also changed how I thought about the afterlife. He helped me see it not as something to fear, but as a place where our connections continue, where spirits can still reach us. Thanks to him, I learned that our loved ones are always close by, and even though we can't see them, we're never truly alone.

"Micky," I said, walking over to him, "I really don't know how to thank you for everything."

He shook his head with a gentle smile, his eyes twinkling like they always did when he had something important to say. "No need to thank me, kiddo. You've got a bright future ahead of you. Just remember, the magic's always been inside you—you just had to see it."

I hugged him, holding onto the warmth and reassurance in his embrace. "I won't forget it, I promise."

As I stepped back, Micky handed me a small, ornate box. "Just a little something for the journey. Open it when you get settled in your dorm."

I nodded, holding the box carefully. "I will. Thanks, Micky."

The sun climbed higher, casting a warm, golden glow over Bayou Vista. Gail, who had become like a mother to me, stood nearby, her eyes filled with pride and love. Her quiet strength and steady support had been my anchor through everything. She had given me the chance to chase my dreams, and I knew I wouldn't be here without her.

She took a deep breath, her eyes misty. "I love you, Loretta," she said, her voice trembling. "Watching you grow and achieve what you've worked so hard for has been one of the greatest joys of my life. I'm so proud of you."

I hugged her tightly, feeling the warmth of her embrace. "I love you too, Mom. I honestly don't know how I would've made it through without you."

Gail gently pulled back, her hands resting on my shoulders. Her eyes shone with unshed tears as she smiled at me, a blend of pride and deep affection.

I looked at her, my heart full. "You've changed my life in ways I can't even put into words. You gave me a home, and your love and support made all the difference."

Gail's smile wavered between tears and joy. "I'm grateful for every bit of it. You've brought so much light into my life, Loretta. Seeing you grow into the person you were always meant to be is more than I ever could've asked for."

We stood there for a moment, letting the warmth of the sun and the closeness between us sink in. It was a quiet, shared understanding—a reminder of how far we'd come together. Gail had become the mother I never had, her love and guidance filling a space in my heart I thought would always be empty. Her presence in my life is something I'll always treasure. She shaped me into who I am today and gave me the sense of belonging, family, and love I'd always longed for.

Coco suddenly bounded into view, leaping into my arms with an exuberant burst of energy.

"I love you too, Coco," I said, my voice trembling slightly as I fought back tears. "Don't worry. I'll be back."

With one last lingering look at the people who had shaped my life, I climbed into my car, the engine quietly rumbling beneath me. As I drove away, the familiar sights of Bayou Vista blurred past, each one bringing a rush of bittersweet memories. There was the old walking path Jill, Tricia, and I used to take home from school—the one nobody goes near anymore since they found Mary Campbell's body buried there. A simple white cross now marks the spot, where her mom visits every day to leave a single red rose. The familiar shops along the streets, the abandoned mill, and the old campground where we uncovered secrets that should've stayed buried.

Roy, my stepdad, lingered in my thoughts like a ghost that refused to let go. The pain he caused shattered my life and tore our community apart. Most of Bayou Vista was convinced he was the serial killer. Everyone, it seemed, except Micky.

It turned out that Micky had been right all along. Recently, women started disappearing again, and the latest cases all seemed to have a connection to Jason's Bar. Micky, now renowned for his ability to communicate with the dead, had garnered quite a following, attracting visitors from far and wide.

He might say he's not anything special, just an old gypsy boy, but to me, he's so much more. To me, he's irreplaceable—a source of strength and inspiration that has touched my heart in ways words can hardly capture. He's my friend, the one who has always been there with a kind word, a listening ear, and a guiding hand. His presence has been a steady anchor in the tumult of life, reminding me of the beauty of true friendship and the profound impact one person can have on another's journey.

As I drove away, Bayou Vista slowly faded in the rearview mirror, but it would never leave my heart. The memories of my time there—the highs and lows, every smile and tear—are etched into who I am. The people who touched my life with their kindness and support are now a part of me.

I plan to return after college with the dream of starting my own business. I want to give back to the community that gave me so much, helping families just like Gail helped me. My goal is to be a source of hope, a guiding light when things seem darkest. I imagine creating a space where people can find the same comfort, support, and inspiration that I did.

When I finally arrived at my dorm and started unpacking, a swirl of excitement and nerves took over. I placed Mr. Teddy by my pillow, just like always. As I sat down on the bed, I remembered the box Micky had given me. Carefully, I opened it to find a small, beautifully crafted heart locket. Inside was a tiny portrait of Micky and me, taken at his shop on one of those afternoons we spent talking and learning.

There was also a note, written in Micky's elegant handwriting:

Dear Loretta,

This locket is a reminder that the magic is always with you. No matter where you go, no matter what challenges you face, remember that you have the strength and the power to overcome anything. The world is full of possibilities, and you have the magic within you to make your dreams come true.

With all my love and belief in you, Micky

Tears filled my eyes as I read the note, a wave of gratitude sweeping over me. Micky's words felt like a beacon, gently guiding me into this new chapter of my life.

I slipped the charm onto my bracelet and then reached for my necklace, holding the familiar pendant tightly in my hand. A deep sense of peace washed over me as I glanced around the room.

Do I still believe in its magic? You bet I do. Not because it holds some mystical power, but because when you believe in something that fiercely, it can change everything.

So, here I am—heart full of memories, future wide open, and ready to take on whatever comes next. Let's see what life's got in store.

Oh, and before I go... I've got a little secret for you. I've already picked the perfect name for the business I'm going to open when I get back to Bayou Vista. Ready? It's going to be called; ***Heavenly Wishes*** - Pretty fitting, right?

A Note From The Author

Dear Readers,
   Thank you for choosing to read *Heavenly Wishes*! I hope you enjoyed the journey as much as I loved bringing it to life. If you'd like to stay updated on all my upcoming releases or even have the chance to become a character in one of my stories, be sure to follow my Facebook page. I truly enjoy connecting with my readers and hearing your thoughts, so feel free to reach out and say hello!

facebook.com/AuthorCarolACampbellGhostStories

I hope you enjoyed *Heavenly Wishes* as much as I loved writing it! If the story resonated with you, I'd be truly grateful if you could take a moment to leave a review. Your thoughts mean the world to me, and your support helps other readers discover my books. Thank you for being part of this journey, and I can't wait to hear what you think!

Thanks!
Carol